"First, you tell me—have you remembered who you are?"

Jane's pulse hammered at the distrust in his voice. "No, why? Do you know who I am?"

Fletch shrugged. "Jacob received a missing-persons report on a woman matching your description."

Jane's breath stalled in her chest. She sensed she wasn't going to like what Fletch had to tell her. "What is my name?"

Fletch released a weary sigh. "The woman's name is Bianca Renard."

Jane shifted, mentally repeating the name in her head. Bianca...that didn't seem right.

In fact, Jane felt more like her name than Bianca.

Fletch remained silent, studying her with hawklike eyes. "Does the name sound familiar?"

She slowly shook her head. "Not really. What else did he say about this woman?"

Fletch pulled a hand down his chin, drawing her gaze back to his beard-stubbled jaw and those lips that had kissed her. For a moment during the kiss, she'd forgotten she was in danger. She'd felt safe.

She didn't feel safe anymore.

LEFT TO DIE

USA TODAY Bestselling Author

RITA HERRON

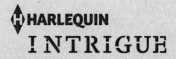

HARLEQUIN
INTRIGUE

To Dotty Graves for being a fan! Happy reading!

HARLEQUIN®
INTRIGUE®

Recycling programs
for this product may
not exist in your area.

ISBN-13: 978-1-335-13568-1

Left to Die

Copyright © 2020 by Rita B. Herron

All rights reserved. No part of this book may be used or reproduced in
any manner whatsoever without written permission except in the case of
brief quotations embodied in critical articles and reviews.

This is a work of fiction. Names, characters, places and incidents
are either the product of the author's imagination or are used fictitiously.
Any resemblance to actual persons, living or dead, businesses,
companies, events or locales is entirely coincidental.

This edition published by arrangement with Harlequin Books S.A.

For questions and comments about the quality of this book,
please contact us at CustomerService@Harlequin.com.

Harlequin Enterprises ULC
22 Adelaide St. West, 40th Floor
Toronto, Ontario M5H 4E3, Canada
www.Harlequin.com

Printed in U.S.A.

USA TODAY bestselling author **Rita Herron** wrote her first book when she was twelve but didn't think real people grew up to be writers. Now she writes so she doesn't have to get a real job. A former kindergarten teacher and workshop leader, she traded storytelling to kids for writing romance, and now she writes romantic comedies and romantic suspense. Rita lives in Georgia with her family. She loves to hear from readers, so please visit her website, ritaherron.com.

Books by Rita Herron

Harlequin Intrigue

A Badge of Honor Mystery

Mysterious Abduction
Left to Die

Badge of Justice

Redemption at Hawk's Landing
Safe at Hawk's Landing
Hideaway at Hawk's Landing
Hostage at Hawk's Landing

The Heroes of Horseshoe Creek

Lock, Stock and McCullen
McCullen's Secret Son
Roping Ray McCullen
Warrior Son
The Missing McCullen
The Last McCullen

Cold Case at Camden Crossing
Cold Case at Carlton's Canyon
Cold Case at Cobra Creek
Cold Case in Cherokee Crossing

Visit the Author Profile page at Harlequin.com.

CAST OF CHARACTERS

Fletch Maverick—He rescued a woman who'd been left for dead in the mountains. But is she an innocent victim or a criminal on the run?

Jane Doe—With a killer on her trail, recovering her memories may be the only way to find out who's after her now.

Victor Renard—Police are looking for Victor's wife for his murder. And Jane Doe's prints are on the murder weapon.

Halls Woodruff—He insists he knows Jane Doe as Bianca Renard and that he's her attorney. Is he who he claims to be?

Neil Akyrn—This private investigator is found dead in the mountains. Was he murdered because he was searching for Jane Doe?

Otis Rigley—He served twenty years in prison for murdering Jane Doe's parents. Has he come back to kill her now?

Officer Clemmens—He faxed Sheriff Maverick the evidence against Jane, which could send her to jail for murder.

Chapter One

Keep running. One foot in front of the other. Don't stop or he'll get you.

She touched her temple, where blood matted her hair. Her head throbbed. Her memory was fuzzy.

The wind whistled, shrill and violent, through the tall pines, hemlocks and oaks. Tree branches shook and bent, cracking. Thick snowflakes blinded her as they swirled in the darkness.

Where was she? How had she gotten here? Which way should she go?

Why was he after her?

She pawed her way through a cluster of pines. Everything looked the same. Endless trees so close together you couldn't see past them. Snow. Fallen limbs. Wet leaves and brush.

She pivoted, searching for a sign as to how to get to a road.

Nothing but more trees. The mountains rising in front of her.

Footsteps crunched behind her. Twigs snapped.

A limb broke off and hurled to the ground in front of her. She stumbled and tripped over it, grasping for something to break her fall. Her hands hit the rough edges of an oak and bark scraped her already bloody palms. Her knees sank into the foot-deep snow. Her clothes were damp, freezing against her skin.

She had no coat. No hat. No gloves.

Shivering, she looked around for a place to hide. Some place he couldn't find her.

"It's over!" a deep voice shouted. "You can't escape."

No...she silently screamed. She had to get away. Instincts told her he'd kill her if he caught her.

Ice clung to her hands and clothes as she shoved herself up. One foot. Another. She trudged forward. Ahead, a path wound to the left. Up a hill. Maybe it led to the road. Or at least to a shelter. A place to hide.

An animal howled in the distance. A coyote? Bobcat?

Bears also roamed these mountains.

Another foot. Another. Her boot caught in a pile of weeds. Her ankle twisted and she lost her footing. She swayed and clawed for something to hold on to. Her nails dug into the bark of a thin pine, and she hugged it, gasping for breath.

Another howl. Louder. Closer. A wolf?

Trembling, she peered through the trees. There it was. A large gray wolf perched on a boulder ahead, its nose in the air, sniffing. Beady eyes darted across the land, searching for prey.

Terror shot through her. If the man didn't get her, the wolf might.

Forcing herself to remain still so as not to invite an attack, she eased back a step. Clung to the trees. Footfalls light. Another step. Then another. No sound.

Only the shrill wind again, and the wolf pawing at the rock.

Tears clogged her throat. She had to stay calm. Breathe in and out. Keep moving. A few steps more, and she ducked behind a cluster of rocks to hide. Maybe she could wait him out.

But the echo of footsteps crunched ice and brush again. She pushed up to run, but two gloved hands grabbed her. A big body behind her. Rough clothes. The scent of a man's musky odor.

"Let me go." Determined to fight, she raised her arm and swung her elbow backward at an angle, but she missed.

"I warned you that you couldn't escape." Something sharp and hard hit the back of her head. A gunshot followed, ringing in her ears.

Pain ricocheted through her temple. Then the world went black, and she fell into the darkness.

ALL FLETCHER—FLETCH—MAVERICK WANTED to do was enjoy a little bro time and then hit the sack. He'd been working double shifts the last two days. Ever since the big snowstorm had hit Whistler and the mountains, his search and rescue team had been on the clock.

Warnings had been issued. People had been advised to stay in. Cancel their plans for hiking the trails. Stock up on food.

That part the locals had listened to. The grocery stores had run out of milk, bread and bottled water. Battery pack phone chargers, generators, flashlights and batteries had flown off the shelves.

Larry's Liquor store had lines backed out the door.

Still some people refused to stay home. As if the predicted five feet of snow and windchill temperatures below zero was propaganda the meteorologists had fabricated to stir up a frenzy at the stores.

This time the weather forecasters had nailed it, though. Clouds started unleashing snow the night before, and it had been a constant downfall of white ever since.

Trouble was weather forecasters missed so often that people didn't pay attention or just blew them off. School closings for possible snow that turned into rain made the South a laughingstock in the national news.

But this one was for real and had only just begun. Fletch sank onto a barstool at the high top across from his brothers, Jacob, Griff and Liam. He was so bone-weary he could barely muster a smile.

"You look like hell," the firefighter of the four, Griff, said.

"I feel like it, too," Fletch muttered as Liam poured him a beer from the pitcher on the table. Liam was with the FBI.

Fletch's mouth watered as his fingers gripped the mug. The beer was an IPA. His favorite.

Jacob, the oldest of the four and Whistler's sheriff, pounded Fletch's back. "Good work finding those hikers yesterday."

Fletch took a sip from his mug, then snagged a wing from the platter and bit into it. "Glad we found them when we did." He wiped his mouth with a napkin. "Man broke his leg and needed medical assistance."

He reached for his beer again, but before he could take another swig, his phone buzzed on his hip. A quick glance at the number and he cursed. "Work."

His brothers traded grim looks as Fletch answered the call. "A family has been reported missing on the trail," his boss, Captain Hanley, said. "I know you just got off duty, Fletch, but we're slammed. Had two other calls. I need you to come in."

Fletch pushed his beer away, stood and clipped his phone back onto his belt. "Be right there."

"You have to go in?" Jacob asked.

Fletch nodded. "Missing family."

Liam motioned for the waitress and asked her to bring a to-go box and a large sweet tea. "At least take some food with you. I know how these things go."

Fletch accepted the take-out food and tea, knowing his brother was right, then headed to the door.

Thirty minutes later, he was geared up with his pack, and he and two fellow rangers, Todd and Danny, met at the beginning of the trail leading to Whistler Falls, where the family was supposed to be hiking.

"Family's named Patterson. A father, two boys, ages seven and nine," Todd said. "They're from south Georgia."

Where it was sunny and warm. They were definitely out of their element in this frigid mess.

The family's white Expedition was parked in the lot. The Appalachian Trail consisted of over two thousand miles of trails through the wilderness running from Georgia to Maine. Designated spots where hikers began their trek still required parking and hiking in. Throughout the states, lean-to shelters had been built to provide accommodations for emergencies, but were barely pieces of wood nailed together with one side open to the elements.

Experienced hikers carried packs equipped

with tents, food and water, emergency supplies, compasses, maps and tarps they tacked up over the open side of the shelter to ward off the wind when temperatures turned dangerous.

Conditions were dangerous now. He hoped the Pattersons had had the good sense to come prepared.

Danny pointed to the trail map, and they scrutinized it together. The areas had been marked with names and points along the way to guide hikers in planning their route and to keep them from getting lost and walking in circles. After a few miles, the trees and rocks all blended together.

"There are two ways they could have gone to reach the falls from here," Danny said. "East—"

"Or west." Todd gestured to the dark clouds. "Let's divide up."

Fletch nodded. "You guys take the eastern section. I'll head west."

They checked to make certain their radios were working, strapped on their packs, then pulled on gloves and hats and headed in opposite directions.

The temperature was nineteen now and dropping, the precipitation from the night before freezing to ice. More snowflakes thickened the air, making visibility difficult. Protective goggles helped, but the fog of white swallowed the ridges and paths in the distance.

Fletch used his flashlight to illuminate the ground, searching for footprints or signs the family had recently walked this way. An animal print here and there caught his eye, but no human prints.

Every few feet he paused to listen for sounds of voices calling for help, and he yelled out as he climbed the hill. Wind howled from the ridges and peaks, the trees shivering as the gusts barreled through at record speed.

His flashlight lit on something red on the ground. He stooped to examine it and decided it was blood. Could be from an injured animal.

Or a person who needed help.

He aimed his flashlight ahead and noted more blood dotting the snow. Enough to suspect the animal, or human, might be in serious trouble.

Pulse pounding, he followed the blood trail up the incline and around a cluster of hemlocks. A branch lay on the ground, soaked in blood. He scanned the area, listening again. Nothing but the shrill wind whipping through the forest and off the mountaintop.

He panned the light in each direction, then spotted drag marks across the snow. Drag marks mingled with blood.

His radio buzzed. "Located the Pattersons," Todd said, his voice cracking with the static on the line.

"Status?" Fletch asked.

"Nine-year-old sprained his ankle, father has a bum knee, and the other boy is close to hypothermia. We're warming them up, then going to get them back. I've already radioed it in. Medics will be waiting. Meet us at the car."

"No can do." Fletch removed his battery-powered camera from his pack and snapped a picture of the blood trail and the indentations where the body had been dragged. "I found blood in the snow. Looks like drag marks from a human. I'm going to follow it."

"Dammit," Todd said. "I'd help, but it'll take both me and Danny to haul the family down."

"They're our priority now. Get them to safety," Fletch said. "I'll let you know if I find something and need assistance."

"Copy that." Todd hesitated. "Be careful, man."

"Always." None of them liked to leave a co-worker out here alone. But sometimes it couldn't be helped.

Besides, they'd trained for it. And no way could Fletch go home without determining the source of that blood and if it was human.

FACEDOWN IN THE SNOW, she roused from unconsciousness, dazed and confused. A dull throb occupied her head, making the trees spin.

Wind knifed through her. Where was she? What was wrong with her?

She mentally rifled through her fleeting memories for how she'd ended up here. But nothing made sense. Gunshots. Running. A fight. Blood…everywhere.

Her name was… Wait, what was it?

Panic seized her. What *was* her name?

A sob caught in her throat. A foggy blur occupied the space where her memories were stored.

The sound of footsteps crunching twigs and ice echoed somewhere in the distance. Footsteps… He was coming after her again.

This time he'd kill her.

She struggled to crawl forward, but her limbs were too heavy and stiff to move.

Her teeth chattered. Her skin stung from the cold, and her chest hurt as she tried to draw a breath.

The sense that she was in imminent danger overwhelmed her as scattered memories broke through the haze. Someone chasing her. A sharp blow.

She clawed at the ground, fingers digging into the brush and icy ground. Her feet pushed at the surface but sank deeper into the frigid snow. Tears of frustration blurred her eyes, then trickled down her cheeks, freezing on her face.

She had to move. Hide.

But her body wouldn't cooperate. She tried to flex her fingers and grappled for a tree limb, something to help propel her forward. But the branch was too far away. She couldn't give up, though. The cold could be deadly.

Summoning every ounce of strength she possessed, she managed to scoot on her stomach and dragged herself a few feet.

Every muscle in her body throbbed with the effort. Even her bones hurt.

Then a gust of wind shook the trees, sending a deluge of icy snow and more limbs down onto her, and she collapsed.

She cried out for help, but her voice faded into the howling wind. Terror bled through her as she sank back into the darkness.

FLETCH TUGGED HIS hat over his ears as he tracked the bloodspots on the ground. He'd been hiking for over an hour.

Something shiny caught his eye near a tree stump, and he waved his flashlight across the area. There it was. Glittering against the white ground. It was caught in the weeds. He hiked over to it, knelt and dug the object from the fresh snow.

A wedding ring.

Questions needled him as he examined it. A woman's ring. Too small for a man. Silver. What was it doing out here in the wilderness?

Someone could have lost it while camping or hiking.

Judging from the fact that it wasn't buried yet, it couldn't have been here long.

He studied the tracks ahead. More blood. Did it belong to the woman who owned this wedding ring?

Another violent gust of wind snapped tree limbs and sent them flying to the ground. The snow was falling faster, accumulating so quickly that it obliterated the blood trail.

He needed to hurry, or he'd get trapped out here himself.

But the mantra he and his fellow rescue workers lived by reverberated in his head—*leave no one behind*.

If someone was injured and needed help, he had to find him. Or judging from the ring—her.

He jammed the wedding band in his pocket, then set out again. Another mile. Then another. Upward toward Vulture's Point, named so because several suicides had occurred at the spot, the bodies drawing the vultures to the canyon below.

What if he was tracking someone contemplating suicide? She could have dumped the ring and then hiked toward the point. But…if so, why was she bleeding? And what about the drag marks? That indicated there was more than one person…

The storm intensified, snow thickening with each mile, the wind the kind of biting cold that stung your skin and clawed at your bones.

Finally he turned the corner past the boulder marking the rise to the point, and spotted something black. A boot? No, a dark red wool scarf…

Adrenaline churning, he took off running. The thick snow sucked at his boots, but he crossed the area and picked up the scarf. More blood drops. Indentations in the snow that looked like paw prints—no, hands digging.

He was close. He could feel it.

The flashlight fought through the blurry haze, and a minute later, he spotted a body. Facedown on the ground, body half buried in the blanket of white.

A woman.

He jogged toward her and lurched to a stop when he reached her. Long dark hair dotted with snow and ice lay in a tangled mass over the woman's shoulders.

He sucked in a breath and stooped to see if she was alive.

Chapter Two

Fletch gently raked the woman's hair away from her slender throat and pressed two fingers to her neck to check for a pulse. He quickly noted her physical description. Long black hair, pale skin, oval shaped face, high cheekbones. No makeup.

She was a looker.

She wore no hat, gloves or winter coat, though. Regular boots, not snow boots.

She hadn't been prepared for the weather, suggesting she hadn't come out here to hike. Or to kill herself.

Dammit. He didn't feel a pulse.

Her body was so still he didn't think she was breathing. Even if she was alive, hypothermia had set in. Her skin was bluish and ice-cold, and frost formed tiny crystals on the exposed surfaces.

He held his breath as he moved his fingers an inch lower and pressed again. Seconds passed. His heart hammered.

Finally he felt a pulse, low and thready. She was alive. At least for now.

He had to raise her body temperature for her to survive.

That meant moving her to the shelter over the next hill.

Blood mingled with the snow on the back of her head, and he examined the area and found a bruise and a gash. Someone had either hit her or she'd fallen and slammed her head against a sharp rock.

Anger shot through him at the sight of the bruise on her cheek and forehead. A bruise that looked as if she'd been hit. Hard.

Blood streaked her pale pink sweater and jeans, and cuts and scrapes marred her hands and arms. He moved her legs and arms gently to check for broken bones but didn't detect a break. That was something.

Breathing out the cold air, he patted her face gently to see if she'd rouse, but she remained limp, eyelids closed. He eased one eyelid up, then another to check her eyes. Her pupils were dilated. Mouth slack.

"It's going to be okay, sweetheart," he murmured.

The snow continued to pelt them, thickening and swallowing everything in sight. He gently scooped the woman into his arms and carried her toward the shelter. The wind gusts battered him as he walked, knocking him off balance, and he had to tread slowly for fear of losing his footing. If he slipped and they slid down the mountain, it would make things worse.

A few more feet, then he topped the hill and spotted the crude shelter. Anything was better than being fully exposed. Adrenaline pushed him forward, and he made it the last few feet. He eased the woman onto the wood floor in the back corner of the hut.

An angry gust hurled snow inside, and he set his pack down, retrieved the rapid response blankets he kept for emergencies and rushed to cover the woman. After he'd wrapped her in one, he yanked out the tarp and tacked it from post to post to create a wall to shield them from the worst of the elements.

The force of the wind was so strong the tarp flipped upward, but he secured it back in place. Then he raced back to check on the woman. Still unconscious.

Her shallow breathing was barely discernible. How long had she been out in the frigid temperature?

His radio beeped and he snagged it. "Fletch here, come in."

"It's Todd. Medics transporting the Pattersons to the hospital. Your status? Over."

"Found a woman on the trail, unconscious,

suffering from hypothermia. Carried her to Vulture's Point shelter. Over."

"Conditions worsening," Todd responded. "Will send a team of medics your way ASAP."

"Copy that. If it clears and she regains consciousness, I'll bring her down the mountain. For now, going to warm her and treat minor injuries." He paused. "No ID. Have Jacob check missing persons reports."

"Description?"

"I'd guess her age is early thirties. Long black hair. Approximately five-three, maybe a hundred and twenty-five pounds."

"Copy that. Keep in touch."

"Will do. Over and out." He stowed the radio with his gear, then slipped from the shelter to gather limbs so he could build a fire in the built-in fire pit. Then he hurried to collect branches that had been blown to the ground in the snowstorm.

When his arms were full, he carried them back to the shelter and put them inside. He secured the tarp, then arranged twigs and two smaller limbs into the pit. Then he retrieved matches from his pack and lit the twigs. It took several minutes for the wood to catch, but finally it flickered to life. He strategically arranged two more branches on top of the flames, then hurried to check on the woman.

She still lay unmoving, face ghost white, chest barely moving up and down with each breath. He yanked off his coat, pulled the blanket off her, wrapped the coat around her, then covered her with the blanket again.

He blew on the embers to spark the flames, hoping the warmth would breathe life back into the woman. Outside, the wind howled, beating at the tarp and the frame of the thin wooden shelter.

He kept watch over her for an hour, but she was still chilled. Desperate to bring her body temperature up, he stripped her wet clothes and laid them near the fire, then removed his own wet clothing and spread it by the fire, as well.

He used the second blanket to make a bed, then positioned her on top of it, stretched out beside her and pulled the other blanket over them. Rubbing her arms with his hands, he cradled her close, praying his body heat stirred life back into her.

He nestled her cheek against his chest and held her, rubbing slow circles across her back. Exhaustion pulled at him, but he forced himself to stay awake in case she roused or needed him.

The fact that bruises covered her body disturbed him, though, during the long hours of the night. First he had to make sure she was okay.

Then he'd find out who'd hurt her and left her in the woods to die.

HER HEAD ACHED. Her body throbbed. And a tingling niggled at her toes and feet.

But warmth seeped through her, slowly alleviating the chill from her bones. She burrowed into it, desperate to escape the cold.

She struggled to open her eyes, but her eyelids were too heavy and her limbs felt weighted down. Big arms held her against a strong solid wall of muscle, transporting her back to the safest place she'd ever known.

She was seven years old and her father was holding her in his lap. He sipped his morning coffee, the steam rising up and floating in the air. The chicory scent was strong, but her father loved his coffee, so she didn't mind, not as long as they were working the crossword puzzle together.

"Two across, another word for light outside," her father murmured.

She tapped her fingers on the folded newspaper, then bounced up and down. "Sunshine."

He made a show of mulling it over, but his eyes twinkled, and she knew she'd nailed it. A second later, he wrote the word in the boxes and tugged at her ponytail. "You're a smart girl, kiddo."

"That one was so easy." She giggled and hugged him. She loved her daddy so much. Every Sunday, they worked the crossword puzzle together. During the week they did word searches and other puzzles that he brought home. A thousand-piece jigsaw of a mountain lion was spread on their game table now.

They finished the crossword in less than half

*an hour—not a record, but a respectable time—
and then her mom appeared with a picnic basket
that they carried to the river park for the day.*

*She jumped in the icy water and popped up,
shivering, teeth chattering. Her father wrapped
a blanket around her, and they built a fire and
snuggled beside it to watch the flames flicker
orange, yellow and bright red.*

Wood crackled and popped, the heat so soothing that she fell into a deeper sleep.

*Then the warmth dissipated, and she was
twelve years old, back at home with the winter
wind seeping through the eaves of the old house.
It was one of those nights she couldn't sleep and
she'd stared at the ceiling, listening to the rain
ping off the roof and wishing it was morning so
she could climb up beside her daddy and do another crossword.*

*A sudden loud crash echoed from downstairs.
Thunder?*

Then a scream. Her mother.

*Terror shot through her and she froze, listen-
ing again. Another crash. Something breaking.
Her father's shout. "Get out!"*

*Panic bolted through her. Someone was in-
side the house.*

*Footsteps pounded. Her mother's scream
again, shrill and terrifying. Then a popping
sound. A gun!*

Choking back a sob, she scrambled off the

bed and ran into the closet to hide. She closed the door, then made her way through the opening leading to the crawl space. It was dusty and smelly, but her parents stored their Christmas decorations inside.

Tinsel dangled from a cardboard box, and the bag of bows her mom stuck on packages sat on top. The bag had gotten ripped somehow; red, green, gold and silver bows dotted the floor like colorful candy.

Another gunshot echoed from down below. Then a clunking sound as if someone hit the floor.

Tears blurred her eyes, and she hugged her knees to her, fighting back a scream. If someone was inside, she had to be quiet or they'd find her.

Her mind raced. Dad had a gun. He kept it locked in the drawer in the kitchen. Had he shot the intruders?

Footsteps pounded again. A door slammed. A car engine rumbled outside.

Then suddenly everything went quiet.

Too terrified to move, she rocked herself back and forth, waiting for her father and mother to tell her it was safe to come out. Tears streamed down her cheeks, but she buried her sobs in her arms.

It was hours later, and still no one had come. The house echoed with a creepy quiet, making her stomach churn. Finally she gathered enough courage to tiptoe downstairs. Her foot hit something sticky and wet on the bottom step.

Then she saw the dark crimson color. Blood everywhere. Splattered on the walls, the staircase, the carpet...

A scream died in her throat. Shouldn't touch the blood. Mom and Dad...they were on the floor... Arms sprawled, legs twisted, eyes bulging wide...

Her own eyes jerked open. God... She'd been dreaming. Or had she?

The suffocating darkness gave way to a sliver of light seeping through a thin wall of wood. She was lying on a hard plank floor. A blanket over her.

Then... A man beside her. Not just a man. A naked one.

She lurched to a sitting position and scrambled backward, dragging the blanket with her.

Where in the hell was she, and what was going on?

FLETCH INSTANTLY SAT UP, pulling his coat over his lap. Dammit, he couldn't help his morning erection.

But he had kept his hands to himself during the long cold night. He'd never take advantage of a vulnerable woman and this one was about as vulnerable as he'd seen. Bruised, battered and near dead. Maybe at the hands of a man.

And if the wedding ring belonged to her, the

man who'd hurt her and left her for dead might have been her husband.

Her eyes widened in horror as she looked at him, then down at herself, then anger flashed across her slender, pale face.

"Who are you?" she said, fear and bewilderment lacing her soft tone. "And what do you want?"

He raised his hands in a gesture meant to alleviate her fear and forced his voice to remain calm. "My name is Fletch. I work with Whistler's Search and Rescue in these mountains." He watched her for a reaction. "Last night my coworkers were looking for a family lost in the storm, then I saw blood."

A war raged in her eyes. Should she believe him or was he some sort of pervert who'd abducted her for evil purposes?

"I followed the blood trail and found you collapsed, facedown in the snow, unconscious. You were barely breathing. Looked like you'd been beaten up, and you'd sustained a blow to your head."

Her eyes darted to her hands, which were still stained with blood. Then she lifted her fingers to her temple and touched the cut on her forehead. "You did this?"

His jaw hardened and he shook his head. "No. Like I said, I found you and brought you here because I couldn't carry you down the mountain during the blizzard."

She clutched the blanket to her in a white-knuckled grip. "So why am I naked?"

As much as he detested the accusations in her voice, he was glad to see she had some fight in her. Probably the only way she'd survived.

"You were suffering from hypothermia. Your wet clothes made it impossible to raise your body temp." He gestured toward the fire. "After I carried you to this shelter, I built a fire and tried to warm you. Shared body heat is the fastest way to accomplish that."

He let the statement stand for a minute, then he stood to retrieve his pack. She gasped at the sight of his naked body in the firelight.

He should apologize, but it was too late. She'd seen him. He'd seen her. What the hell was the big deal?

He dug in one of the pockets of the pack and removed his ID.

When he looked back, fear darkened her eyes again as if she'd expected him to draw a weapon. He offered her his picture ID.

"See. I'm a ranger, Search and Rescue. My job is to find missing and lost people in the mountains and bring them home safely."

Her hand trembled as she examined his badge, and she glanced from his photo back to him, scrutinizing both.

"I'm sorry for frightening you," he said, then knelt and stoked the fire again. "I radioed in our location, so we'll either hike out when the snow lets up or they'll send a team in when they can."

Her breath rattled in the frigid air. "You saved me?"

He gave a humble shrug. "That's my job."

A tense silence stretched between them, and he checked their clothes to see if they were dry. Thankfully, they were, so he yanked on his jeans and shirt, then carried her clothes to her.

"All dry now."

Her gaze met his, questions still lingering, but at least she wasn't screaming or running. She motioned for him to turn around. A sly grin lit his face. He'd seen her naked, but that was different.

Besides, he wanted to win her trust. "I'll be right back." He slipped through the tarp opening, secured it, then walked into the woods to collect more kindling.

Deciding to give her privacy, he scanned the area, but the snow was still falling in thick sheets of white, now knee-deep. The wind was brutal, the windchill factor below zero.

It would be dangerous to set off down the mountain at this point. Best to let the worst pass.

He rubbed his hands together, then gathered more sticks for the fire, ducked back inside the shelter and reattached the tarp.

"Can we leave now?" the woman asked.

Firelight illuminated her milky white skin and throat. Her bruises looked more stark this morning, the dried blood on her forehead a reminder that she'd sustained a head injury.

"Not yet, snow's still coming down hard, and the windchill is well below zero." He dropped the sticks by the fire in a pile, then added a few more to keep it burning.

Then he pulled two bottles of water from his pack and carried one to her. "Here, drink. You need to stay hydrated."

She looked at him warily but accepted the bottle, unscrewed the cap and took a long swallow.

He pulled a granola bar from his pack and handed it to her, then took one for himself. Although he forced himself to eat only half, he let her finish hers before he spoke. Then he sat down in front of her and offered her a gentle smile.

"Better?"

"Thanks." She tugged the blanket back over her as if it offered a sense of security.

"I told you who I am," he said gruffly. "Your turn now."

She clamped her teeth over her bottom lip and glanced down at her bloody hands.

"Your name's a good start," he said. "I can radio my team and let your family know you're safe."

Her gaze rose to meet his, pain and confusion clouding the depths.

His stomach clenched as protective instincts

kicked in. "Hey, it's okay." Keeping his distance, he gestured toward the bruises on her hands. "I didn't hurt you. So tell me your name and who did this, and I'll make sure the police find him and put him away."

Chapter Three

Distrust niggled at her as she studied Fletch. His ID looked genuine, and so did the concern on his face.

But she'd been running from someone and couldn't remember who or the man's face. IDs could be faked.

What if he wasn't who he claimed to be?

She clutched the blanket he'd given her, her mind racing. Although if he'd wanted to kill her, why hadn't he left her out in the elements? Why warm her and offer her food?

Another few hours outside, and she would have died. Unless he wanted something else…

"Listen to me," he said as if he realized her train of thought. "I didn't touch you last night, except to wrap you up and treat you for hypothermia. I know you're scared and that someone hurt you. Talk to me and I can help."

She rubbed her temple where her head throbbed, searching desperately for details of the past few hours. Or days. How long had she been out here?

He stood, retrieved something from his bag, then set it in front of her. A radio.

"This is how my team communicates. I'll call them and prove that you can trust me."

She wanted to trust him but said nothing. She was bruised and battered. Common sense warned her to be cautious until she figured out what was going on.

A grim look settled in his eyes, but he picked up the radio, pushed a button and spoke into it. "Ranger Maverick, Search and Rescue, unit 9. Come in."

Static rattled over the speaker.

"Come in," he repeated.

More static, then a voice, but it was garbled. "Dammit, the storm's creating too much interference," Fletch muttered.

He tried it several more times, even walked to the edge of the shelter to see if he received better reception, but nothing.

"I'm sorry," he said with a shake of his head. "We'll try later when the storm lets up. I called our location in last night, though, so my team knows where we are."

He was trying to comfort her, but her nerves raged all over the place.

With a weary sigh, he sank down by the fire and stoked it again. "If I was in your shoes, I wouldn't trust me, either," he murmured. "But I swear on my mama's grave I'm not going to hurt you." He gestured toward the bruises. "And I sure as hell didn't do that."

His tone was so convincing and protective that she relaxed slightly.

"Now," he said again, "please tell me your name."

A cry of frustration lodged in her throat, but she swallowed it back. "I… I don't remember."

FLETCH NARROWED HIS EYES. "What do you mean? You don't remember your name?"

Her tangled hair fell in a curtain over her injured temple and the bruise on her right cheek. She'd obviously suffered abuse or been attacked. Or maybe she had taken a fall.

Fear darkened her eyes. "I don't remember what happened or how I ended up in the woods." She rubbed her arms with her hands and scooted nearer the fire. "How can I not know who I am?"

Fletch gave her a sympathetic look. "You sustained a head injury. The gash on the back of your head probably caused you to lose consciousness and may be messing with your memory."

She lifted a trembling hand and traced her fingers over her head, then winced when she made contact with the knot on the back. "You're right. It's probably that." She exhaled. "But I don't recall how I was injured." Her voice trailed off, tinged with misery and fear.

Fletch inched closer to her, then took her hands in his. Her nails were broken, dirt and blood beneath the surface. Maybe there was DNA from her attacker. "It looks like you fought with someone. Do you remember an altercation? If someone attacked you?"

A frown marred her face as she examined the particles beneath her nails. "You're right. That is blood." She pushed her sleeves up, studied the bruises on her arms and the discoloration circling her wrists, and her frown deepened.

"Those bruises around your wrists look like rope burns," Fletch pointed out.

She lifted the blanket and glanced at her ankles. "My feet were tied, too."

Emotions darkened her eyes, and she dropped her head into her hands and made a low sound in her throat. "God, maybe I was kidnapped."

"That's a possibility." Which meant her kidnapper might still be in the woods, trapped in the storm. Or on the lookout to make sure she was dead.

She looked so lost and terrified that instincts whispered for Fletch to pull her into his arms and comfort her. But that would be out of line.

"Listen, you're safe now," he said calmly. "Until you remember your name, we'll call you Jane. Is that okay?"

"Like Jane Doe," she said matter-of-factly.

"Yes, unless you want to be called something else."

She massaged her temple. "No, Jane is fine."

"When the blizzard lets up, we'll call for medical help," Fletch said. "For now, let's assume the blow to your head caused some sort of temporary amnesia. Once the swelling goes down, hopefully your memory will return." He paused. "Until then, you need to rest."

"So you're a doctor now?" she asked wryly.

Fletch cleared his throat. "No, but my job requires EMT training."

She rubbed her arms more frantically. "How can I rest when I don't even know who I am?"

"Maybe talking would help jog your memories," he said. "Tell me anything you recall. Something about your childhood? A face? Your favorite food?"

She twisted her fingers around the blanket. "I was dreaming. I think it might have been a memory."

Fletch held his hands over the fire to warm them. "Go on."

"I was about seven, and I was sitting on my father's lap," she said. "It was Sunday and we were in his big comfy chair by the fire."

"Sounds like a happy time," he said. "Do you remember your father's name? What he looked like?"

She pinched the bridge of her nose as if searching her mind. "No, but we always did crossword puzzles together. That and other puzzles. We were working on a thousand-piece one of a mountain lion. I saw the pieces spread out on a table. Then my mother packed a picnic and we went to the river for the day."

"Sounds like you grew up in a loving home," Fletch said with an encouraging smile.

The worry lines bracketing her slender mouth softened. "That was a good memory. But…" Her voice broke. "But later… I had a different dream… I think my parents are dead."

Fletch sighed. "I'm sorry. What happened?"

Pain wrenched her face. "I… Someone broke into our house and shot them."

A tense second passed. "Do you think their murders are related to what happened to you now?"

She blew out a ragged breath. "I don't think so. If my dream was real, it was years ago. I was only twelve."

"That's tough for a kid." Sympathy for her filled him. "Who did you live with after you lost them?"

She murmured a sound of frustration. "I… don't know. After that, the rest is blank."

Another tense moment stretched between them. Fletch understood the pain of losing parents. He missed his every damn day. Sometimes when he was hiking, he thought he heard his father's voice telling him the names of the trees and where the best fishing spots were. Other times he could hear his laughter echoing in the wind as if he was a little boy, and his father was chasing him and his brothers in the backyard. Their black Lab, Tag, ran in circles following them.

And his mother…in the kitchen baking. Humming beneath her breath. Her hot chocolate in the winter and her insistence on family dinners. Her hugs and smiles every night as they went to bed. The notes she'd put in their lunch boxes when they were in grade school…

But today wasn't about him, so he cleared his throat. "How about other family?" he asked. "Maybe a grandparent or sibling? Perhaps they filed a missing persons report."

Another frustrated sound escaped her. "I…don't know. Maybe."

"You didn't have any ID on you when I found you, so I asked my team to have my brother to look for missing persons reports based on your description. He's the sheriff of Whistler. I'm sure they're working on it now."

That seemed to relax her, and she leaned back against the wall.

"There's something else," Fletch said.

"What?" Her voice took on an edge. "You know something you aren't telling me?"

He removed the ring from his pocket, then

held out his palm, the wedding band nestled in the center. "I found this not far from where you were lying." He searched her face. "Does it belong to you?"

JANE'S VISION BLURRED for a moment as she studied the wedding band. Simple white gold, tiny diamond chips embedded in the band.

Not fancy or expensive. No large ostentatious diamonds or other precious stones.

Exactly the type of ring she felt like she would choose.

Although what did she know about herself?

Fletch eased it into the palm of her hand. "Look at it. Maybe it will spark some kind of memory. If you're married, your husband's name, the venue or city where you held your wedding… any detail might help."

Emotions thickened her throat as she ran one finger over the smooth band. The inside of the shelter suddenly blurred, the room swaying, and she clawed at the floor to remain upright.

Then an image. A man's large hand. Rough and calloused. Short clipped nails. Olive skin. A tattoo of a wolf on the underside of his arm.

Long nimble fingers sliding the ring on her left hand. Her wiggling her fingers as she looked at it, testing its weight, measuring how it felt to be married.

She jerked her head toward Fletch, something

akin to panic knifing through her. "It's mine," she whispered.

He didn't react. Simply watched her with a calm expression. He knew how to be patient. Listen.

Extract answers.

Was he really with Search and Rescue, or did he have a police background?

"Jane, what do you remember?"

"A man's hand, sliding the ring on my finger."

"So you are married?"

She fought a wail of panic. "I suppose so. But all I saw was a hand, not the man's face." She stood and paced across the small dimly lit space. "I can't believe this is happening."

"Just give it time," Fletch said gruffly. "Things will come back to you when you're ready to remember them."

"What about until then?" she cried.

"Until then you rest and regain your strength while we wait out the storm."

She folded her arms across her middle. She needed to talk about something else. Something besides herself. "All right. Tell me about you. Do you have a wife? A family?"

He chuckled. "No, not me. But my brother Jacob just got married."

Her legs still felt weak, so she sank onto the floor beside him. Firelight flickered across his strong, angular face, illuminating eyes that were a deep chocolate brown. His hair was dark, thick, shaggy, and at least two days' worth of beard stubble grazed his jaw.

For a moment, her stomach fluttered. Fletch Maverick was handsome in a rugged, alpha male way. He could be dangerous.

But he carried you to safety.

Maybe she *could* trust him…

"Do you just have the one brother?" she asked to fill the silence.

He pulled a wallet from his back pocket, then removed a photograph and showed it to her. "There are four of us. Jacob's the oldest, sheriff of Whistler. That's the closest town."

He'd mentioned him before. And Whistler? Had she been there?

He gestured toward the photograph. "That's Griff. He's a firefighter. And Liam's with the FBI."

"You're all first responders." All ruggedly handsome, dark hair, big bodies, muscles, arresting eyes. Especially Fletch's. She could swear he was probing into her soul with those dark chocolate orbs.

"Yeah." He ran a hand through his hair, spiking the jagged ends.

"Impressive," she murmured.

He shrugged, his shirt stretching across muscles that she'd felt when she'd nestled in his arms during the depths of her nightmares.

"My father was sheriff of Whistler," he said, his voice quiet as he looked into the flames. "Five years ago, a horrific fire at the local hospital tore the town apart. Dozens of people were injured, and there were casualties. My father ran in to help and didn't come out alive."

Jane barely stifled a gasp. "I'm sorry, Fletch. That must have been horrible."

"It was." Pain streaked his face. "Jacob was Dad's deputy back then and decided to fill Dad's shoes after he was gone."

A second passed, wood crackling and popping in the silence. "What started the fire?"

"Arson," Fletch said. "Bastard who set it was never caught. That drives us all. Every time I'm on the trail, I'm on the lookout for the arsonist in case he's living off the grid in these mountains."

A shudder coursed up Jane's spine. "The mountains are a perfect place to hide."

His troubled gaze met hers in the glow of the fire, tension simmering. "He destroyed a lot of lives. We won't give up until we find him and make him pay."

She wanted to reach for him, touch his hand. In the quiet of the shed, his promise and the loneliness in his voice tore at her heart. Made her feel close to him, as if they shared a bond.

But firelight flickered off the wedding band, and she knotted her hands in her lap.

The ring was hers. She remembered that. And a man had given it to her.

But a wedding…vows…the man's face…were all lost in the void that now filled her mind.

Fletch had suggested the head injury caused her amnesia. But traumatic events could cause loss of memory, too.

Keep running. One foot in front of the other. If you stop, he'll get you.

Then his voice. You can't escape.

What if the man she'd married was the one who'd been chasing her in the woods? What if she'd been trying to escape an abusive relationship, and her husband was the one who'd hurt her and left her for dead?

Chapter Four

Jane's head throbbed as she struggled to sift through the dark blankness in her mind.

If she was married, was her husband looking for her? Or had he hurt her?

Domestic cases were rampant. Abusive men could be charming. Chameleons who looked handsome in one light and changed their colors in another. Had her husband disguised himself as a good man until their wedding, then revealed a sinister side after the honeymoon was over?

She closed her eyes, desperate to see his face or hear his name, but the effort cost her and intensified her headache. Agitated, she stood and walked over to the doorway of the lean-to. She eased the edge of the tarp open and peered outside.

A sea of white filled her vision, the heavy downpour of snowflakes across the land obliterating any signs of greenery. The sky was a smoky gray and the wind howled like a sick animal, adding to the dismal feel.

Fletch was right. It was too dangerous to hike in this blizzard.

For some reason she didn't understand, she instinctively felt she could trust him. His voice was smoky, gruff, layered with concern and tenderness. And when he'd described his family, emotions tinged his eyes.

Although how could she trust a virtual stranger she'd just met when she obviously had doubts about the man she'd married?

For a brief second, a shadow filled her vision and the world slipped out of focus. Then faces drifted through the fog coated air… *A man and woman and a child. Laughter, then the man picked up the little girl and swung her around. The woman stooped, gathered snow in her gloved hands, then threw a snowball at them. The little girl laughed and giggled, then the man and girl made snowballs and laughed and shouted as they had a snowball fight.*

Jane tensed, her breathing choppy as she realized there was no one in the snow. That the image was a memory from her childhood. A sense of peace enveloped her that she had had loving parents and a happy home.

Until they'd been murdered.

The realization made her chest ache as if she'd just lost them that second. Maybe because it felt like yesterday or maybe because it was the only real memory she could hold on to.

Why could she remember a part of her childhood and not her name or her husband's or how
she'd ended up out here in the storm, bloody and
bruised?

A noise startled her, and a large branch broke
and tumbled to the blanket of white on the
ground. Then another shadow.

An animal maybe? A wolf? Mountain lion?
Bear?

There it was again. The shadow. A movement…

What if it was the man who'd hurt her? Maybe
he'd hung around to make sure she was dead…

FLETCH STOKED THE fire as he watched Jane at the
door to the shelter. She was obviously struggling.
How would it feel to wake up with no memory
of your name or your life?

Although some things he wanted to forget, like
the day his father died. Talking about his family reminded him of the huge hole in his heart
left by his father's death. In his mind, he saw the
last few minutes they'd talked. They were having coffee at the diner when the call about the
fire had come in.

They were joking about the local high school
football game and the quarterback who'd put
Whistler High on the map with his record stats.
Fletch's mother was home making her famous
pot roast with the baby carrots and peas that he

and his father requested once a week. Griff had asked for peach cobbler for dessert. Liam wanted her biscuits. And Jacob her sweet tea.

It had been an ordinary day. A hint of impending rain in the air, but no sign that Whistler was about to experience the worst tragedy in the history of the town.

Then the call… *His father leaped up immediately, told him about the fire. Fletch wanted to ride with him, but his father said he'd meet him later at dinner. Neither one of them had any idea how serious the situation was.*

Sirens from the fire truck raced by. Griff was on duty, so he would probably be late for dinner just like his father. He decided to keep his mother company till then.

So Fletch paid the bill while his father jumped in his car and raced to his death.

Pain and guilt squeezed at his lungs. If only he'd stuck with his dad, maybe he could have saved him…

Two hours later, just as his mother pulled the peach cobbler from the oven, Jacob called. He'd barely been coherent and said it was mass chaos. They needed more manpower to help evacuate patients from the hospital. Some might be trapped.

Fletch and Liam left their mother to keep the food warm while they drove like maniacs to the hospital. Just as Jacob said, the scene was chaos.

Hospital patients in wheelchairs and on gurneys filled the parking lot. Staff members struggled to get out while tending to the needy. Firefighters raced in, geared up, to rescue victims and evacuate the building while other firefighters worked to extinguish the blaze and keep it from spreading. Screams and cries echoed from terrified staff and patients.

As soon as they parked, they hit the ground running and dove in to help. The heat from the blaze seared his skin. Flames burst into the night sky like an orange fireball. They had to hurry.

The next half hour he and his brothers helped carry the injured and sick outside.

Then Jacob emerged, shouting their names. He was pale and panting as he dragged their father out of the inferno.

Jane made a startled sound, jerking Fletch from the depths of the tragic memory. She clenched the tarp edge, her eyes wide.

Fletch hurried to her. "What is it?"

"I thought I saw someone," she whispered. "A shadow moving. Maybe a man."

Fletch urged her behind him, then peered out into the storm. Trees bent and swayed in the throes of the turbulent wind gusts, and snow swirled in a hazy sea of white.

She was right. Fletch saw the shadow. Something moved about a hundred feet away. His body tensed, senses honed as he searched the wilderness.

Wait… There it was. A movement again.

The bruises on Jane's body taunted him. If the person who'd hurt her was still out there, he might have tracked them here.

Fletch rushed to his pack and removed his pistol. Jane's eyes widened as she watched him, fear glittering in the depths. He lifted one finger to his lips in a silent gesture to keep quiet.

He carried the gun with him to the door of the shelter, braced it at the ready and waited.

FOR A MOMENT when Fletch retrieved his gun, Jane froze in fear. But the protective gleam in his eyes when he urged her behind him gave her a sense of safety. At least she wasn't facing this situation alone.

"Do you see anything?" she whispered behind him.

"A movement," he murmured. "Can't tell what it is yet. Could be an animal or a hiker who got caught in the storm looking for refuge."

Which meant he would help them.

Only the tense set of Fletch's shoulders indicated he was prepared for trouble.

Tension vibrated in the small confines of the lean-to, Jane's worry rising with each passing second. If only she could remember what happened to her, she could give Fletch insight as to her attacker's identity.

And if he might still be looking for her.

The blizzard raged on, visibility worsening as the precipitation thickened. Fletch suddenly stiffened and tightened his fingers around his weapon. He'd seen something.

Jane searched the thick snowdrifts, anxiety needling her. An image of a gun in her hand suddenly flashed behind her eyes. A second later, the image disappeared as quickly as it had come, leaving her confused.

And with more questions.

Did she know how to use a gun? Did she own one?

The few things she'd remembered about her father taunted her. He hadn't been a violent man and she didn't recall him hunting, yet he'd kept a gun locked in a drawer in his study.

She closed her eyes and willed a mental picture of him to surface. His study, the big chair by the fire where they worked the crossword puzzles. Wall-to-wall bookcases held leather-bound books. She raked her gaze over the shelves, trying to decipher the titles. Had he liked novels? Mysteries? Were they nonfiction books?

She massaged her temple again, and saw the words *Law Review* on the spine of a large black book.

Was her father a lawyer?

Fletch shifted beside her, and she opened her eyes. His shoulders relaxed slightly, and he heaved a breath.

"What is it?" she whispered.

"Bear. She's moved on up the mountain." He pointed to a ridge in the distance. "Probably looking for a place to hibernate."

A chill went through Jane. "Do you think she'll come back here?"

"Could, but I doubt it. Looked like a mama. Saw a cub farther up the trail, so she went toward her baby."

Relief softened Jane's fears, and she walked back to the fire and sat down on the blanket again. Adrenaline waning, exhaustion took over.

"You okay?" Fletch asked.

He remained at the door, gun in his hand, like some kind of rugged lawman. But his eyes pierced her with worry.

"Just a headache, and I'm tired," she said softly.

"Lie down and sleep a while. I'll keep watch and wake you if the storm lets up."

His gruff voice was so comforting that she murmured thanks, then succumbed to fatigue and stretched out, wrapping the blanket around her. Firelight flickered, the kindling popping in the quiet of the shelter. Yet outside, the wind howled, brutal and deadly.

Knowing Fletch was watching over her, she closed her eyes and let sleep claim her.

But in her sleep, the nightmares came. *The blood... She was running... Death was near. She couldn't escape it...*

FLETCH KEPT WATCH by the doorway, ears alert for sounds of someone approaching.

He tried his radio again as the hours passed, aware each time Jane startled awake from a bad dream. Her sleep was restless, as if she was fighting off her demons—or her attacker all over again.

Late afternoon, Jane roused, mumbling incoherently. She shouted no, then opened her eyes, trembling as she looked around the shelter. She was still lost in the nightmare, her eyes glazed, her hands clawing at the covers as if she needed to hide beneath them.

"Shh, it's all right, you're safe now," Fletch murmured.

At the sound of his voice, Jane turned her head toward him.

"It's Fletch, Jane. You fell asleep and were dreaming."

She inhaled deeply, chest rising and falling with her labored breathing.

"I found you in the snow, collapsed. Do you remember me?"

She slowly nodded, then shoved her tangled hair from her face.

"Did you remember something else?" he asked.

For a moment, her eyes looked blank, then finally she shook her head.

"I'm going to gather more wood, and then I'll make us something to eat."

She didn't speak, so he decided to give her a few minutes to acclimate. He stowed his gun in the waistband of his pants, removed the small pot he carried in his emergency pack and stepped outside. He scanned the land as he left the shelter, then collected more sticks for the fire. He set those inside to dry, then dipped some snow into the pot.

The wind force was so strong that snow had blown across the land and formed knee-deep drifts. His face stung, the fog so thick he couldn't see three feet in front of him. A noise made him jerk to the left and reach for his weapon, but it was only a large branch breaking off in the wind.

He hurried back to the shelter, anxious to make sure Jane was okay. He sensed she'd remembered something, but she hadn't wanted to share it.

When he entered the shelter, he found her hunched beneath the blanket, watching him warily.

"I tried the radio again, but it's still down," he said softly. "Hopefully the storm will let up by morning and we can get through." He set the pot over the fire on the grate, then fastened the tarp again.

While the snow melted and the water began to boil, he retrieved two packets of dried soup mix from his bag along with two tin mugs. He dumped the soup mix into the mugs, then poured water over it and stirred. He carried Jane a mug and she reached for it, her hand shaking.

"I figured you were hungry. You need to eat to regain your strength."

She licked her lips. "You're prepared."

He shrugged. "That's what I do." While she sipped the hot soup, he sat down by the fire and did the same.

An eerie quiet settled through the shelter. The sound of their breathing mingled with the raging wind outside that beat at the lean-to.

"You want to talk?" he finally asked.

She heaved a breath and shook her head. "I'm just tired."

Concern filled him and he rose, walked over and gently touched her forehead to see if she had a fever. Her skin felt cool, though.

"Mind if I look at that gash on the back of your head? I'd like to clean the wound to prevent an infection."

She murmured permission, and he retrieved his first aid kit from his bag. She set her empty mug on the floor and turned her back to him. He gently eased her hair away from the wound and wiped the blood with alcohol wipes. She winced slightly when he touched it, but as he cleaned it, he realized it wasn't as deep as he'd first thought.

"Looks like it'll heal on its own," he said. "Not so deep you need stitches."

"That's good," she said softly.

"Yeah." The emotions in her voice made him want to squeeze her shoulder for comfort, but he stepped back. "You cried out in your dreams," he said. "What was that about?"

Her eyes widened, and she turned back to look at the fire, then tugged the blanket around her again. "I was running from a man, but I still couldn't see his face."

"Was that all?"

She nodded, then leaned her head onto her knees. Fletch studied her, his jaw tight.

Why did he have the sense she was lying to him? That she'd seen something she didn't want to tell him about?

Chapter Five

Jane paced across the shelter to avoid eye contact with Fletch. She had had crazy dreams while she slept, bits and pieces of a jumbled life and images triggered by her fears.

At this point, she didn't know what was real and what wasn't.

A corkboard hung on the wall on the far end of the small shelter, an assortment of handwritten notes and messages tacked onto it that visitors had left to mark their stay or to pass on to others hiking the trail.

She studied the board and the crude messages, listing dates and times people had sought refuge from the elements, or when they were just weary from hiking the miles and miles of wilderness. Most who planned to hike from Georgia to Maine gave up somewhere along the way.

The terrain, weather conditions, long days of isolation and the physical exertion were too difficult. Enthusiasm for adventure waned as injuries and illness occurred, bitter cold set in, and insects and rodents infested the lean-tos with dangerous bacteria. Longing for hot showers and warm food intensified as the monotony of trail mix and dried food became increasingly harder to endure.

One message caught her eye. A note with dried flowers shaped into a heart. She smiled at the thought that a couple might be leaving each other love notes along the way.

She closed her eyes, willing images of her husband to surface. If he hadn't hurt her, then maybe someone else had, and her husband was searching for her.

Hands knotted, she scanned the others and noticed another one, more cryptic. *I'LL FIND YOU.*

Her heart hammered as her attacker's words echoed in her mind, and she looked down at her hands. Blood still stained her skin and darkened her fingernails.

"Jane, are you all right?" Fletch's gruff voice broke into her thoughts.

She hated living in the dark. She wanted answers. If she wasn't trapped here, she'd go to the police. What would they do?

"We probably should take samples under my nails to give to the police when we get out of here, in case I scratched my attacker."

Fletch's brows rose. "I thought about that, but I didn't want to do so without your permission."

Her gaze met his, and for a moment doubts set

in again, kidnapping cases taunting her. If Fletch had attacked her, he could have brought her here and pretended to take care of her to win her trust.

She'd heard of kidnappers keeping victims in seclusion until they developed Stockholm syndrome.

"Jane?"

She frowned, wondering why that thought had occurred to her. Logically her theory made sense, but when Fletch examined her wound, his touch had been gentle, not harsh like a man who'd ever hurt a woman. If Fletch had wanted to kill her, he could have left her in the woods to freeze to death.

The radio buzzed, a sound that startled her in the silence.

Fletch jumped to his feet and hurried toward his radio. He tapped the receiver. "Fletch here. Over."

A rattling sound. More static.

"Fletch here. Can you hear me?"

"Todd. Checking on your status."

"Holding our own at the shelter. News?"

"Blizzard supposed to pass around four a.m. Warming tomorrow."

Jane sucked in a breath. Once the snow stopped and the temperature rose, they could get off the mountain.

What would happen then?

"About the missing woman, Jacob called."

Fletch glanced up at Jane. "Go on."

"Said…" A sudden gust of wind snapped the air, the sound of tree limbs falling outside thundering as limbs crashed against the shelter.

"Todd?"

"S…" Static crackled and popped, cutting off the man's voice.

Fletch made several more attempts to reconnect but failed.

A frisson of nerves danced along Jane's spine. Jacob was Fletch's brother, the sheriff of Whistler.

Had he learned her identity?

FLETCH SILENTLY CURSED as the radio died again. Dammit. Jacob might have figured out Jane's identity or if she had family looking for her.

Knowing who she was might lead them to answers about her attacker.

He tried the radio again, but static popped and the connection failed.

Exhaling in frustration, he decided to wait a little while before making another attempt. At least his team knew their location, and for now, Jane was safe.

"You were right about your nails," he said quietly. "There might be DNA there."

She stretched her hands in front of her and studied them. "I do want to know," she said, although fear laced her voice.

He removed a small tool and a baggie from his

pack, then walked over to her. Her eyes flickered with unease at the sight of the tool.

He offered it to her. "You can do it if you want."

Relief echoed in the breath she exhaled. "No. I…trust you."

Their gazes locked for a brief second, heat flaring to life in the dim confines of the shelter. The days were shorter now, and night was already setting in. He stooped down beside her, then eased her small hand in his. Her fingers were long and slim, her nails broken and jagged from the attack. Her ivory skin looked pale in contrast to his bronzed skin, her hand soft and delicate next to his calloused one. Her eyes bored into his for a second before she broke eye contact.

She was a beautiful woman. Her features were put together in a sexy kind of way, her eyes a pale startling green. At the moment, they were intense and full of pain and questions.

A hint of sexual awareness tugged inside him, heating his blood.

Dammit, not the time. He had to wrangle his libido under control.

Focusing on his task, he lifted one finger of hers, gently eased the tip of the tool beneath her nail and scraped particles of dried blood and dirt. Hopefully there were skin cells from her attacker, too.

When he finished, he handed her sanitizing wipes to clean her hands.

She thanked him, then used another wipe over her face and throat. The slender column of her neck was smooth but marred with a bruise as well, as if someone had tried to strangle her. He hadn't noticed it before, but now the discoloration was showing, handprints evident on her skin.

Son of a bitch. Only a coward would hurt a woman.

Fresh anger shot through him at the thought. Strangulation could have dangerous aftereffects not recognized at an initial examination.

She propped her back against the wooden wall of the shelter, drew her knees up and leaned her folded arms on them. "Tell me more about your family," she murmured.

"Not that much to tell." Fletch had never been a talker.

"Please," she said. "It helps distract me."

He heaved a breath, struggling for what to say.

"Do you have any leads on that arsonist you mentioned?"

"Not really. A woman named Cora Reeves gave birth to a baby girl the night of the fire. Her baby was kidnapped, so we suspected the fire was a diversion by the kidnapper to allow him time to escape."

Jane's eyes widened. "Was it?"

Fletch shook his head no. "Cora and her husband divorced, but she stayed in Whistler. She never gave up looking for her daughter."

"I don't blame her. Did she find her?"

A small smile tugged at Fletch's mouth. "Yeah, a few months ago. She thought the little girl living down the street was her child, and got my brother involved. Turns out she was right."

"So who stole Cora's baby?"

"A woman named Hilary… She was in love with Cora's husband and thought she could break up their marriage if the baby wasn't in the picture. And she was right. Their marriage fell apart, and Cora's husband ended up marrying Hilary."

"Did he know what Hilary had done?"

"No. He was shocked when he learned the truth."

"What happened to the baby?" Jane asked.

Fletch's heart squeezed. "She was adopted. But when Cora started looking at the little girl down the street, Hilary murdered the adoptive mother and tried to kill Cora. Jacob saved Cora and the child, and now Cora has her daughter back." He rubbed his neck. "My brother Jacob married Cora and is raising the little girl."

"So there's a happy ending?" Jane said quietly.

He heard the ache in her voice. Would there be a happy ending for her?

Fletch swallowed hard. There would be if he had anything to do with it.

EAGER TO DISTRACT herself from her problems, Jane probed Fletch for more information about his family.

Although he didn't seem like the talkative type, she managed to convince him to tell her about his childhood, what it was like growing up with three brothers and about life in Whistler.

He told her about Jacob and Cora's outdoor wedding at a small private vineyard, with Cora's little girl standing beside them.

"It was informal," Fletch said. "Cora wanted flowers from her own flower garden, with picnic-style tables for the reception."

A woman's wedding was supposed to be the highlight of her life, yet Jane couldn't recall anything about hers. Remembering even the smallest detail might lead to her husband's name or where they were living. "What about music?"

Fletch shrugged. "I play the guitar a little, so Jacob asked me to play."

Something about his humble admission intensified Jane's attraction toward him.

"I'd like to hear you play sometime," she admitted.

His sexy eyes met hers, but he made no promises. How could he when her mind was a blank slate at the moment? She couldn't move forward with her life until she figured out what she was running from in her past.

"I'll keep trying the radio if you want to rest,"

Fletch offered. "Hopefully, in the morning we can start down."

She twisted her hands together, then snuggled beneath the blanket, curled on her side and closed her eyes. Maybe daylight would bring answers. At least she felt physically stronger now. Her limbs weren't aching as much, and her headache had dulled to a light throb.

As she drifted to sleep, the sound of Fletch's voice as he'd described his family echoed in her head. He'd painted the picture of a loving, close-knit family. He and his brothers met at least once a week for beer and bro night. Sometimes, they worked together, as well.

Her parents were dead, but what if she had a sibling? She strained to remember her childhood again, the picnic, the crossword puzzles, yet nowhere in there did she see a sister or a brother.

Sleep finally claimed her, but her dreams were confusing and scattered. Her father again… *They finished the puzzle, and she climbed down to help her mother bake cookies. Her father's phone rang and she heard his deep voice speaking low into the phone.*

"DA made a deal. Life, no parole."

Her father…was a lawyer? No…a judge.

Then another flashback to that night and the blood again. *Police officers streaming in, snapping pictures. Her parents' bodies sprawled on the floor. Her mother's bloody hand reaching out as if trying to clasp her father's.*

Her father dead, unable to help her.

Next she was looking at more bloody bodies. *A man and woman. Not her parents. Blood spattered the floor and walls. The white comforter and carpet, the woman's hand stretched out as if reaching for her husband...*

Then another couple. *Different faces...different bedroom. A four-poster bed with a lemon yellow spread. Red dotting it and streaking the floor. The woman's eyes bulging in death...*

The images faded and she saw the man with the tattoo on his wrist. *A wolf... His fingers as he slid the wedding ring on her finger. Then his hand clutching his chest as blood spewed... His body bouncing backward, slumping against the wall.*

Her...hand shaking as she gripped the gun...

She jerked awake, lungs squeezing for air as questions pummeled her. Why was she seeing dead people in her dreams? Who were those couples? Was it real?

And the man with the wolf tattoo—her husband. Had she pulled the trigger and ended his life?

Chapter Six

Jane had remembered something. Something that had upset her.

Fletch was sure of it. Her body trembled, and her pupils were dilated as if she was locked in the terror of her nightmares. He'd seen her tossing and turning, heard her mumbling. She'd clenched the covers as if fighting off an assailant.

He'd considered waking her from the horror but had held back, hoping she was remembering details about the man who'd attacked her.

Something to help nail the bastard.

Only now she was awake and sat hunched, knees drawn up, arms wrapped around them, staring into the fire again.

He wanted to push her but sensed that would be a mistake. When the storm lifted in the morning and he reached his team again, Jacob would have some answers, he hoped.

A noise outside startled him, and he went still, listening.

Jane lifted her head. "What was that?"

Fletch mentally sorted through the various noises outside. "The wind and more limbs breaking."

Her breath rushed out in relief, then she turned and stretched out on her side, facing away from him. Fletch itched to go to her and comfort her, but she needed space.

He also wanted to make sure no one was outside.

"I'm going to gather more wood." He settled his gun in the waistband of his pants, pulled on his gloves and eased back the tarp. He scanned the area as he stepped outside. Shivering, he tugged the hood of his coat over his head as he set off to search the area. Snow and wind blasted him, the windchill dipping lower with every hour.

Night had fallen across the land, making it look desolate, as if they were entrenched in a vast wasteland of white. Icicles hung from the tree limbs like jagged knives. His boots crunched frozen snow and brush.

The snow was falling so fast it was burying everything, but about a hundred feet from the shelter he spotted an animal's paw prints. Thankfully they were leading away from the shelter, toward the north. He wove between a cluster of trees and detected more prints ahead.

They were partially destroyed by the blizzard conditions, but these appeared to be human.

From his earlier treks on the trail, he'd discovered a few loners who lived in the woods off the grid. Some he suspected were simply homeless or had mental issues and had become recluses.

One guy called himself Homeless Joe. He carried everything he owned on his back, lived off the land and had managed to survive in the hills for ten years already. He lived like a nomad, never staying in one place for long. Another was a man in his sixties who shared a lean-to with his wife of forty years. She claimed she had psychic powers and saw the dead, which made it impossible to live a mainstream life.

Others might be hiding out from the law.

Like the person who'd set the fire that had killed his father.

He kept hoping he'd find the bastard. Although, with no evidence pointing to a specific person, it was possible he'd already encountered him without realizing it.

Fletch aimed his flashlight beam ahead and saw more prints. Too big for Homeless Joe, who was slight-framed and dragged one foot behind him. No pattern of his gait here.

He forged ahead, checking each direction, then heard a noise. Icicles snapped and cracked, breaking off and flying through the air. He dodged them, then hiked toward Crow's Point. Another noise, and he paused. Then he spotted another print. Large.

Definitely human. Judging from the indentation in the snow, boots.

A man's.

Dammit. Did they belong to someone else stranded out here, or to Jane's attacker?

JANE WOKE THE next morning to the sound of Fletch entering the shelter. He'd stayed out late last night, then come in looking troubled. When she'd questioned him, he'd claimed he was just tired, that he'd seen a shadow, but it had turned out to be a wild animal.

She shivered as he boiled water and made them some instant coffee. His beard stubble added to his rugged appearance, making him look as if he belonged to the mountain.

He was probably just as untamed and wild in bed.

Good heavens. She shouldn't be thinking about his sex appeal now.

"Sorry, coffee's not very good," he muttered.

"At least it's hot," she said, although she would kill for a latte.

He handed her a breakfast bar and she forced herself to eat it slowly. It hadn't escaped her that Fletch had been rationing them. "Thank you for everything," she said softly. "If you hadn't rescued me, I wouldn't have survived."

He shrugged as if it was no big deal. "Just doing my job." Closed inside in this tiny space with the firelight flickering off his face, she almost felt safe, as if a killer wasn't chasing her.

He ate his bar and sipped his coffee, then tried the radio again. Static popped, and his jaw tightened. But several seconds later, he managed to connect to his team.

"Weather conditions?" Fletch asked.

"Storm has definitely moved on. Winds dying down, temperature rising. Should get above freezing by noon."

Jane massaged the back of her neck, anxious to return to civilization. Even more anxious about what she might learn.

"Do you need us to send a team for you and the woman?" Fletch's teammate asked.

Fletch motioned to Jane. "No, we can manage. Will radio you if we require assistance."

"Take the trail southwest," the other man advised.

"Copy that." Fletch hesitated. "Did you hear anything else from Jacob?"

"Yeah. He's searching missing case reports across the state. He wants an update on your status."

"Tell him we're fine for now."

"For now? Is there trouble?"

"The woman was injured," Fletch replied. "Not sure if her attacker is still around, but will be on the lookout."

The men agreed to stay in touch, and Fletch turned to her. "We're probably about eight miles from the entrance point to the trail near Whistler. I know you're still weak. Do you think you can make it at least partway?"

Jane stood and stretched. "Yes, I feel stronger now." She just had to find the courage to face the truth about who'd attacked her. And why she saw those bodies in her sleep.

Fletch encouraged her to drink some water. She did as he said while he packed up his supplies, removed the tarp and stowed it. Then he handed her a pair of gloves, a hat and his coat.

"I can't take your jacket," Jane said. "You'll freeze."

He pulled a thinner, insulated jacket from his bag. "I'm used to it. Now, if you start feeling weak or lightheaded, let me know and I'll call for reinforcements."

"I'll be fine, Fletch."

When she stepped outside, the blast of cold hit her. She zipped Fletch's coat and bounced on her heels to warm her muscles, then followed him. He cut away limbs, moved branches and alerted her when they reached rocky terrain. Her boots were slick and inappropriate for blizzard conditions, but she grabbed tree limbs and rocks to steady herself.

With each step they took, she was moving closer and closer to civilization.

And to the truth.

A foul odor wafted toward her as they wound

around a patch of hemlocks. Vultures swooped down ahead, diving toward the ground.

"Must be a dead animal," Fletch said. "Let me make sure."

She stayed close behind him, holding on to his hand to keep her balance as they descended the steep hill. They reached a ledge, and Fletch threw his arm out to prevent her from stumbling forward.

A second later, she spotted the bloody animal down below.

"Dead wolf," Fletch said.

An image of a wolf perched on a boulder searching for prey niggled at her memory. *She was falling into the snow, thought he was going to get her.*

Then a gunshot.

She startled as if she'd heard the sound that second.

"What is it?" Fletch asked.

"The man… I was running and fell," she said breathlessly. "He came up behind me and shot the wolf." Her voice cracked.

"He saved you from the wolf?" Fletch asked, confusion tingeing his voice.

"I don't know if that's what he meant to do. But he grabbed me from behind, and a second later, I heard a gunshot. Then I passed out." She lifted her fingers to the back of her head. "The gun…he hit me with his gun."

"Did you see what kind of weapon he was carrying?" Fletch asked.

She shook her head. "No, but the bullet whizzed so close to my head that for a moment, I thought he'd shot me."

She paused. "I don't understand that. If he wanted me dead, why *didn't* he just put a bullet in my head?"

FLETCH CONTEMPLATED JANE'S STATEMENT. If the man wanted her dead and he was armed, why *hadn't* he shot her? His mind ticked away different theories.

"Perhaps he didn't want to leave evidence behind. Bullets can be traced back to a specific gun. With the blizzard bearing down, he expected you'd die in the elements, then no one would suspect murder."

Emotions darkened her eyes. "That makes sense."

Although it still left questions unanswered.

"You okay to keep going?" Fletch asked.

Jane nodded, and he set off on the trail again. Although he knew the woods and stopping points along the way, it was still easy to get turned around in the midst of the sprawling miles of forest. He consulted with his map and compass to guide them.

Fletch gestured toward a path that wound

straight downhill and looked treacherous. "That's the fastest way, but too dangerous."

Jane remained silent, her face a mask of concentration as they fought through the thick brush and dodged clumps of falling snow from the trees. The wind shook limbs and more branches broke off, but the precipitation had slowed to a light snowfall, and the temperature was warming as sun peeked through the spiny branches.

In spite of the cold, Fletch began to sweat as they hiked. He paused at the end of each mile to check Jane's physical condition, and encouraged her to drink water to stay hydrated.

He led them toward the right on a slightly less steep hill, but they had to tread slowly to maintain steady footing. Jane's boots were slick on the bottom, and she slipped a couple of times, so Fletch helped her along the steeper patches.

Another half mile and they reached a lean-to at the point called Stone's Ledge. "Let's take a break and rest a minute," he told Jane.

She followed him to the shelter, although she hesitated at the opening and clutched the wall. Her face turned ashen, her breath puffing out in a hazy cloud.

"What's wrong, Jane?"

"This place," she murmured. "It seems familiar."

He retrieved his flashlight and stepped inside. He spotted a pile of rope in one corner along with a bloody rag.

She heaved a breath. "He brought me here," she said in a ragged whisper. "That rope…he tied me up and gagged me and left me."

Fletch breathed out. "What else do you recall?"

"Being dragged through the snow. I was hurt and drifting in and out of consciousness. When I came to in the cave, though, I was alone."

"So he left you in a shelter instead of outside," Fletch commented, confused again.

"I think so." She stepped inside the dank space. An odd look crossed her face as she walked over to the corner where the rope lay. "When I came to, I didn't know where I was. Just that I had to escape."

"Then what happened?"

Jane crouched down and ran her hand over the floor, then closed her eyes and rubbed at her temple. "I untied myself, then I heard something outside. He was coming back."

Various scenarios played in Fletch's mind. None of them good.

Why had her attacker brought her here? To hold her for ransom?

Her parents were dead, although she could have other family…

Fletch's stomach clenched. The other possibilities were even more sinister.

The man could be some psycho who got off on sexual assault or torture…

JANE CURSED HERSELF for not being able to remember more details about the man who'd hurt her.

"I'm going to photograph the scene, then bag the rope and rag," Fletch said. "Hopefully the lab can retrieve your attacker's DNA from them."

Jane ran her finger around her wrist where rope burns discolored her skin. In her mind, she pictured herself working the thick rope, slowly loosening the knots.

Her fingers were aching, bloody, her nails ripping as she yanked the knot free. She had to hurry. He could come back any minute. She ripped the gag from her mouth, then tackled the rope around her ankles. The rope slipped, her nail breaking, and she cried out in frustration.

Shh, *she told herself. He might hear you.*

"Jane?"

Fletch's voice shattered the memory like glass breaking.

"Are you ready to go, or do you need to rest?"

A shudder coursed up her spine. She didn't want to stay another minute in the place where she'd been held captive. Dried blood had crusted on one of the wooden boards where a loose nail stuck out. She must have used the nail to saw the ropes and cut them.

Fletch pulled something from his pocket and tacked it on the bulletin board. An article about the Whistler Hospital fire. Then he wrote the words *I'LL FIND YOU.*

So he had left the message she'd noticed before.

His expression was grim. "I've been putting these in all of the shelters. If the arsonist is hiding along the trail, I want him to know I'm looking for him."

"I don't blame you." She tugged the cap over her ears and stepped from the lean-to. "Let's get out of here."

Fletch stowed the baggie holding the rope and rag in his pack, then joined her outside. The wind had died down slightly, and icicles were starting to melt and drip from the tree branches.

Jane forced herself to concentrate on the terrain as she followed Fletch down another steep hill. They wove between massive tree trunks and climbed over fallen limbs and branches.

Another half mile, and they reached a sharp ridge overlooking a canyon with views of the snowcapped mountains. "This is beautiful," she murmured.

Fletch's jaw tightened. "My father used to bring me and my brothers up here camping during the summer. He's the one who first taught me wilderness survival."

"You must miss him a lot," Jane murmured.

"Every day," Fletch admitted gruffly. "All the more reason to track down the person who set that fire and make them pay."

"You'll find whoever it was," Jane said. Fletch

was the kind of man who did what he said. The kind of man a woman could count on.

Had her husband been that kind of man?

They hiked around a turn past a large boulder. The sound of brush bristling came from behind them. Someone was back there.

Fletch motioned for her to take cover. She started toward the rocks, and Fletch snatched his gun from the waistband of his pants. Before he could pull it, a gunshot echoed and a bullet whizzed by her head.

Jane ducked and Fletch pushed her forward. She hit the ground on her knees just as another gunshot rent the air.

Fletch dove behind her with a grunt. A second later, she realized he'd been hit.

Chapter Seven

"You're hurt," Jane gasped as she crawled behind the boulder.

"Just my leg. Stay down." Fletch reached for his gun. He'd dropped it when he'd fallen and it had skidded into the bushes by a cluster of rocks.

Another bullet pinged off the ground near them, and Fletch yanked his hand back. Blood was pooling in the snow like a red river. He looked slightly disoriented, the color draining from his face.

Panic seized Jane. What if the bullet had struck an artery?

Jane's heart hammered. She was closer to the gun, so she rolled sideways to her stomach, dug her hand in to pull it from the weeds. Footsteps crunched the frozen ground behind her, and the man jumped her before she could snag it.

She swung her elbow backward and jabbed him in the solar plexus. He cursed, slapped her across her temple and crawled on top of her. Jane bucked and fought him, shoving with all her might until she managed to push him off her. She crawled toward the gun, but he grabbed her by the neck and dug his fingers into her throat, choking her.

She elbowed him again and used her foot to kick at his legs. Her nails dug into his hands as she struggled to pry his fingers from her throat. But he increased the pressure, and she saw stars.

She refused to let this maniac kill her. Fletch needed her…

Rage clawed at her, and she summoned all her strength and jerked the man's hands from her neck. Fletch groaned. He tried to push himself to his knees but collapsed. He was weak, but he heaved for breath, and dragged himself toward her.

Her attacker jerked her upright by the shoulders and slammed her back against the jagged rock. Pain ricocheted through her, and her head snapped forward.

The world spun, and Fletch grabbed at the man. The man loosened his hold just enough to send a swift kick to Fletch's wounded leg. Fletch bellowed in pain. Blood spewed, and he collapsed face down in the snow.

Jane had to move quickly. She rolled sideways, snatched the gun from the bushes and raised it at the ready. Her hand was trembling, the world tilting at an angle. She blinked to focus and pressed her finger on the trigger.

The shooter suddenly lunged toward her, raised his weapon and fired. But she was quicker. She rolled sideways to dodge the bullet, aimed Fletch's gun straight at the bastard and released a round. The bullet pierced the shooter between the eyes. Brain matter and crimson red spewed from his head and spattered the white snow.

His body flew backward, and he slipped over the mountain ledge and spiraled downward into the canyon below.

FLETCH STRUGGLED TO open his eyes.

He heard a strangled sound and glanced around for Jane. She'd crawled to the edge of the ridge and was looking over. Dammit, was she shot?

"Jane!" he called. Was she all right? He'd slipped in and out of consciousness while she fought the bastard.

And she *had* fought.

Questions mounted in Fletch's mind as the last few minutes replayed in his head. She not only had fought, but her maneuvers looked practiced. Trained. She also knew how to handle a gun like a pro. Had she grown up with guns? Could she have served in the military? Or was she in law enforcement?

"Jane?" Fletch called again.

His voice must have finally registered, and she looked at him with a glazed expression. She lowered the gun by her side as she walked over to him and knelt.

"Are you all right?" he asked.

She nodded, eyes wild with shock. "He's dead."

"Did you recognize him? Was he the man who hurt you?"

"I...don't know," she said in a ragged whisper.

Fletch lifted a weak hand and squeezed her arm. She was shaking from adrenaline. "You had no choice," he said in case she was starting to experience guilt. "It was self-defense."

"I know." Her breath rattled in the air. A moment later, she straightened, snapping out of the shock. "We need to take care of your injury." She reset the safety on his gun and stowed it in his pack. Then she dug inside and found a first aid kit. She removed a bandage strip and tied it around his leg to stem the bleeding.

"Let's move you to a shelter so I can take a better look at your wound," Jane said, all businesslike.

She was right. Blood might draw a wild animal. "I'll radio for help when we're inside." His strength was waning with the blood loss, but he was determined not to pass out again. At least not until they reached the shelter. She might be strong, but she couldn't move dead weight.

She helped him to stand and slid her arm around his waist. His pride smarted, but he wasn't stupid. They had to depend on each other for survival.

He leaned on her as they trudged toward the shelter. "It's about a half mile," Fletch said as he pointed the way.

"Can you make it?"

"Don't worry, I'll be fine." Fletch ground his teeth against the pain as they hiked. One foot in front of the other.

The pace was slower than before, and he kept an ear alert for another gunman.

Jane lapsed into silence, a look of fierce concentration on her face. Her tenacity and courage were probably the reason she'd survived so far.

Finally they managed to reach the shelter, and he stumbled inside. He detested being weak, and willed himself to remain alert in case the gunman had an accomplice.

Jane clamped her lips together as she retrieved his emergency medical kit. She handed him his radio while she retrieved scissors. He connected the second go around.

"Fletch. Headed down the mountain with Jane Doe. Ran into trouble. Gunman attacked. Took a bullet to the leg. Jane Doe is okay for the moment. Over."

"Damn, Fletch," Todd said over the line. "How seriously are you injured?"

"Some blood loss, but I'll make it. The bullet didn't hit a major artery. Over."

"We'll send a med team to you ASAP. Unfortunately all teams are out on calls. This blizzard wreaked havoc on the trail. A group of teens were trapped north of Pigeon's Peak, and we dispatched units there to dig them out. Small plane went down in the eastern area, so teams have been sent to rescue them. An avalanche west of Whistler caused multiple injuries and more victims are thought to be trapped."

Fletch bit the inside of his cheek. Jane was watching him with a worried expression as she cut away the leg of his jean where he'd taken the bullet. The fabric was soaked in blood, snow and dirt.

"Inform Jacob about the gunman. His body is just south of Stone's Ledge. Shot in self-defense." He didn't point out that Jane had done the shooting.

"Copy that. Keep me posted," Todd said. "If you need emergency airlift services, let me know."

"Will do." Fletch disconnected and set the radio down while Jane examined his wound.

He propped himself up on his elbows to give himself a better view. "How deep is it?"

She twisted her mouth sideways. "Not too deep. Maybe a couple of inches."

"You need to remove the bullet," Fletch said.

Jane shook her head in denial. "I'm not a doctor. At least I don't think I have medical training."

"You don't need it." Perspiration trickled down

his neck. "But you heard my team. They can't get to us yet. If we leave the bullet, there's a chance of infection. Then I won't be able to walk out of here."

Or walk again. He sure as hell didn't want to lose his leg.

Jane planted her hands on her knees and inhaled sharply. "Fletch, I…don't know if I can do it."

Fletch bit back a moan of pain. "I saw the way you fought off that man," Fletch said. "You handled yourself like a pro, Jane. You also knew how to shoot a gun."

Her face blanched as if he'd said something wrong.

"It's not a criticism," he said. For God's sake, he needed to soothe her nerves. She'd just been attacked and killed a man. Even a professional would be shaken.

"If you can do that, you sure as hell can dig a little bullet out of my leg."

Emotions glittered in her eyes, then she lifted her chin. "All right. Just tell me what to do."

Fletch patted her hand, determined to keep her calm. For now he needed her help. Later, they'd talk about how she'd learned to fight and shoot.

JANE MENTALLY BRACED herself to remove the bullet. Fletch had saved her life twice now. How could she refuse his request?

Yet the image of that man as she'd shot him haunted her. Who was he? Why had he tried to kill her?

Would her memory return, or would she be forever lost in this suffocating emptiness?

"Look in the first aid kit," Fletch instructed. "There's a knife and tweezers in there along with antiseptic wipes. There's also a vial of alcohol to sterilize the knife with. And you can heat it over the fire."

Perspiration beaded on her skin as she removed the supplies and built a fire.

"What about an anesthetic?" Jane asked.

"I don't have one." He reached underneath his flannel shirt and ripped off the tail end of his T-shirt. "I'll bite on this. Now make a small incision beside where the bullet is lodged, then use the tweezers to pull it out."

Jane wiped sweat from her forehead. He made it sound easy. And she had just killed a man. But he had been trying to kill her and Fletch. She'd acted in self-defense.

Hurting Fletch was different. She didn't want to cause him pain. He was strong, caring, protective. If he hadn't saved her, she'd be dead.

Fletch touched her hand. "Look at me, Jane."

Her breath caught at the tenderness in his eyes. "You can do this. Remember you're helping me. It'll be over in no time, then we can both rest."

The shooter's face taunted Jane. Who the hell was that man? Did she know him?

Fletch closed his eyes as if he was losing consciousness. "It's time, Jane. Let's get it over with."

He was right. No sense stalling. Besides, she wanted and needed Fletch to survive.

She quickly sterilized the knife blade and tweezers. Then she cleaned the area around the wound, allowing her a clearer picture of what she was dealing with.

"Are you ready?" she asked.

He looked pale now, his complexion pasty. "Do it, Jane. You've got this." He stuffed the T-shirt strip between his teeth and bit down.

Focusing on the task, she gripped the knife and surveyed the opening where the bullet had pierced his thigh. Deciding that acting faster was better than drawing out the pain, she quickly pierced his skin with the knife. His body stiffened, his jaw tightening. She leaned closer and quickly dug around the bullet.

He groaned, sweat beading on his skin, but she forced herself not to look at his face. *Just do it*, he'd said.

And she did. She steadied her hand, then concentrated on extracting the bullet. Blood gushed from the area, and she wiped it away with another sterile wipe, then tugged on the bullet with the tweezers until it slipped free from where it was embedded. Her hand trembled as she dropped the bullet into a plastic bag she'd found in Fletch's pack.

Wiping perspiration from her forehead with the back of her arm, she cleaned the wound again and glanced at Fletch. He'd passed out during the extraction.

She had to finish. She found thread and a needle in his bag, cleaned the wound again, then slowly stitched together his skin to close the opening. When she was finished, she dressed it with a gauze pad and wrapped it with tape to secure the bandage.

Relieved that part was over, she sank back on her heels and inhaled several deep breaths. Fletch was unconscious now and needed rest before he could attempt to hike again. Maybe his team would finish their other missions and come after them.

Until then, she'd take care of Fletch the same way he'd taken care of her.

Afternoon came and went as Fletch slept. He shivered and moaned, a fever working through him. She mopped the sweat from his forehead with a cloth she found in his bag, wetting it with melting snow to cool his skin. She shook a couple of painkillers from the bottle in his bag and gave them to him.

He slipped in and out of consciousness, occasionally whispering her name, and she stroked his arm to comfort him. "I'm here, Fletch."

"Gun," he mumbled. "My gun."

"It's in your bag."

"Keep it close," he murmured. "Case you need it."

She tensed at the reminder. Fletch had protected her with his life.

If someone else came after her, she'd protect them both.

Night was setting in, and she finally succumbed to fatigue and stretched out beside Fletch. Knowing he was next to her gave her a sense of peace and safety, yet she kept guard in case of another attack.

But then she dozed off and the nightmares came again. *The blood... A woman's face staring up at her in death. A man sprawled beside her, his chest gaping open with blood soaking his shirt.*

She rolled over, struggling to escape the nightmare. Not her parents this time. *No...the face was a young woman, the man lying next to her with his hand stretched toward her as if together they'd found death.*

She jerked awake. Why did she keep seeing these dead people in her mind?

Her parents' murder, her husband's...the man chasing her...the man she'd shot...

Were they all connected?

Chapter Eight

Jane surveyed the woods from the shelter's door. In the aftermath of the blizzard, the wind had died down and the forest seemed eerily quiet. Shadows seemed to move and slip away, the tall trees obliterating the moonlight.

No more hiking until Fletch was better. He needed rest and time to regain his strength.

She tacked the tarp over the opening, co-cooning them into the small space and shielding them once again from the elements. Her stomach growled, a reminder they hadn't eaten since morning, and she found some trail mix in his pack.

She settled by the fire and allowed herself to eat a handful, saving some for Fletch when he woke. Occasionally he called out to his father as if he was reliving the past, then he'd open his eyes and look around in a daze.

She understood that feeling. The past haunted him. It haunted her, as well. Except she'd lost most of it and she wanted it back.

Jane cradled his hand in hers. "It's night, Fletch. We're safe here until morning."

He blinked as if confused, then recognition flickered in his eyes. "How long have I been out?"

"A few hours. I removed the bullet and bandaged your leg." She wiped his forehead with a damp cloth. "Hopefully tomorrow you'll feel better."

"Have to get you out of here." He used his elbows to prop up, but she gently coaxed him to lie back down.

"You need to rest. It's dark now."

"You have my gun?"

She patted the pocket of her jacket. "It's right here."

"Where did you learn to shoot?" he asked, his voice breaking as he fought sleep.

Jane racked her brain for the answer. "I don't know. It just came instinctively."

"Because you've had training," Fletch murmured. "And you can fight…"

Jane massaged her temple. "Maybe I took self-defense classes. Or… I think my father had a gun. He must have taught me."

Fletch's brows furrowed, and he blinked as if trying to stay awake. Then slowly his lids closed and he succumbed to the fatigue. Jane patted his shoulder, then checked outside again. Thankfully she didn't see anyone lurking around or hear sounds of an intruder.

Her head ached, so she returned to sit by the

fire beside Fletch and keep vigil. If his fever spiked higher, she'd use his radio to call for help.

The night loomed long and cold and lonely, though, and eventually when he was resting peacefully, she stretched out beside him again. Her bones felt chilled from the cold, so she crawled beneath the blanket and curled close to him.

Fletch was right. Shared body heat definitely was better than going it on your own. His big muscular body radiated such warmth, strength and power that it lulled her into a sense of safety. She suddenly wanted to tell him everything.

"Fletch," Jane said softly.

"Yeah."

"I don't know if it's important, but I've been having a recurring nightmare. Maybe it's a memory. I don't really know." She rubbed his back, needing comfort. "I keep seeing dead people in my mind. Couples who've been murdered. I… don't know if it's real or not."

Different scenarios raced through her mind. Maybe those faces belonged to a story she'd seen on the news. Or…maybe she was a journalist who'd covered the murders. Or…maybe she knew one of the victims personally…

Or…what if someone wanted her dead because she'd witnessed one of the murders?

FLETCH FLOATED IN and out of reality. Haunted by his father's death and the fire that had stolen his life, for a minute he was back in Whistler. He and his brothers were breaking the news of his father's death to his mother. He felt helpless as she fell apart. Chaos in the town followed over the next few days as reality hit. Numerous people were dead. Cora's baby was missing. Shock spread as police revealed that someone had intentionally set the fire.

He jerked himself from the tragic memory, his body shaking with emotions. Behind him, a warm body touched his.

"Shh, it's okay, Fletch."

A woman's voice. Soft. Her fingers caressed his back in a soothing gesture.

He turned toward her. Wanted her closer. To feel her comforting arms.

Soft breasts pressed against his chest. Her breathing turned erratic. A leg wove between his.

His heart pounded, heat flaring inside him, and he drew her closer. Couldn't help himself. It had been a long damn time since he'd been with a woman. Since he'd allowed himself to let down his defenses.

Since he'd felt so needy.

Part of him didn't like it. Yet her breath bathed his neck, and he couldn't stop himself. He pulled her tighter against him, then lowered his head and closed his lips over hers.

Hunger seized him, and he moved his mouth across hers, seeking, tasting, savoring the sweet touch of her lips. She returned the kiss, stroking his calf with her foot as his tongue explored her hungrily. He threaded his hands through her hair and tilted her head back to taste the sensitive skin of her neck.

She made a low sound in her throat, then pressed kisses on his jaw and cheek as she tunneled her fingers through his hair. He moaned and rolled her sideways to climb above her when a pain shot through his leg.

At the same time, she flattened her hands on his chest. "Fletch, wake up," she whispered. "We can't do this."

The sound of her voice startled him back to reality and out of the depths of his dream. Only he wasn't dreaming.

He'd been kissing Jane.

Her eyes were doe-like in the dim firelight, her mouth parted, lips red and swollen from his kiss. Silently cursing, he pushed himself off her and rolled to his back a few inches away.

"Dammit, Jane, I'm sorry." He scrubbed a hand over his face, half delirious from the desire still pumping through him.

The air became charged. Heated.

"I can't believe I did that," Fletch murmured. "I…was dreaming. But…that's no excuse." Maybe on some level he'd known exactly what he was doing.

And that he was doing it with Jane.

But he'd crossed the line. Jane was a married woman with amnesia.

A woman he was supposed to keep his damn hands off and protect.

JANE TURNED AWAY from Fletch and pressed her fingers to her lips. She could still feel his sexy mouth moving over hers, feel his hands stroking her hair and back. Feel his thick length pressing against her belly.

He had been asleep.

She'd been asleep as well, lost in the throes of memories that threatened her sanity.

One moment she'd dreamt about a suburban neighborhood where she'd gathered with friends. The men were grilling burgers while the women spread side dishes and desserts across a picnic table. While the meat barbecued, she sipped wine and chatted with the ladies who were discussing the latest book club pick.

The houses were traditional, owned by thirtysomething married couples who shared common interests and a neighborhood swimming pool where the children laughed and played in the summer.

Diamond chips sparkled on her wedding band in the sunlight as she'd reached for her wine glass.

Only nowhere in the picture did she see her husband.

She certainly didn't remember climbing in bed with him at night.

Loneliness permeated her soul, and she'd felt Fletch's arms around her. She hadn't been able to resist his warmth and comfort.

But it was wrong. Kissing Fletch when she knew nothing about herself except that someone wanted her dead.

What if the couples at that neighborhood gathering were the ones murdered?

"Jane? I'm sorry," Fletch said again.

She shook her head. "You don't have to apologize, Fletch. We were both half asleep." She lifted her chin and turned to face him. "Nothing really happened, so let's forget about it."

His gaze latched with hers, questions and doubt darkening his eyes. She wished she could give him the answers he needed. The ones she craved herself.

"I'll be right back." Needing fresh air, she grabbed the tin Fletch had used to melt snow in for coffee, stepped outside and studied the desolate terrain. Thick layers of white still blanketed everything in sight. Tree limbs hung heavy and bowed beneath the weight of frozen ice. Melting snow dripped from branches and puddles had begun to form, turning the frozen ground into a slushy mess.

Early morning sunlight fought through the treetops and slanted rays across the ground and rocks. She gathered enough snow to melt for coffee and some more small twigs and branches, then carried them inside.

Fletch had managed to sit up and was digging through his pack. She made quick work of adding the twigs and sticks to the fire, then stoked it and set the tin of snow on top. They worked silently but in tandem and made coffee. While they sipped it, she warmed her hands over the fire.

"Last night, you mentioned something about couples being murdered." He studied her over his coffee. "What was that about?"

She traced her finger around the rim of the tin mug. "I was dreaming. I don't know if what I saw was real or nightmares. Everything's all jumbled in my mind."

He remained silent for a moment, the air between them filled with a sensual awareness she didn't want to feel for Fletch. One she couldn't act upon, not again.

She might as well talk it out. They'd be back to civilization again soon, and his brother, the sheriff, might be able to fill in the blanks.

"I dreamed about murders," she said. "I saw faces of women and men who'd been killed, pictures of their bodies all bloody and ghostlike as if I was there. I don't know if I saw them on the news or if there's more to it. If it was real and if it's connected to me."

Fletch's eyes darkened. "Did you recognize any of the victims?"

She massaged her temple where a headache pulsed. "No, although in another dream I saw myself at a neighborhood barbecue in the suburbs. There were couples there."

Fletch leaned forward, his expression earnest. "Was one of the victims at the neighborhood gathering?"

She closed her eyes, struggling to discern the faces, but everything was blurred, filled with scattered bits that didn't fit together like different puzzles where the pieces had been mixed up.

"I...don't know, Fletch." She raised her head and looked into his eyes, terrified of remembering.

Terrified of not.

FLETCH STRUGGLED TO shake the memory of that kiss from his mind. But it was damn hard.

Especially when he looked at Jane's vulnerable expression and wanted her again.

"It's a good sign that you're starting to remember things," he said. "Those bits and pieces may not make sense now, but eventually you'll figure out what it all means."

She bit her bottom lip, her eyes filled with doubt. "I was thinking, Fletch. What if someone showed up at that dinner party and murdered my friends?"

He narrowed his eyes. "You mean a mass shooting?" He ran a hand through his hair. "That would certainly be traumatizing. I don't recall hearing anything about a mass shooting at a neighborhood barbecue recently, and that kind of thing makes national news. But I can ask Jacob to explore that angle. It might be a lead."

"The man I shot could have been the shooter, and he wanted to silence me because I witnessed the murders."

"That's a possibility," Fletch said. If it was a triggering event, it might give them a timeline for how long Jane had been held captive. And with the evidence he'd collected, it might lead them to a name.

Although if the man had committed multiple murders, he obviously had no conscience, so why hadn't he shot Jane and ended her life, too?

Fletch eased the bandage on his leg away from his wound to examine it. Jane had stitched up the incision like an expert. The wound was clean, no signs of infection.

There was definitely more to Jane than what was on the surface.

Jane's hair fell in a curtain over her cheek as she checked the incision. He had the insane urge to push it away from her face and draw her back to him for another mind-blowing kiss.

But that would be stupid. And unprofessional. Suddenly anxious to get them off the mountain, he sat up. Another night with Jane alone and he might give in to his attraction toward her.

He needed to consult with his brother. If a mass murder had occurred as Jane suggested, Liam might be working the case.

Jane handed him a fresh bandage, and he applied it while she packed up the supplies and extinguished the fire. He gritted his teeth and pushed to stand, testing his weight on his leg. Surprisingly it held up.

"Are you sure you can walk?" Jane asked, her voice filled with concern. "You could call your team to send medics after you."

He damn well did not want to go down the mountain on a stretcher, not unless he had to. His team was needed elsewhere.

"I'm fine." He raised a brow. "My gun?"

She gestured toward the floor beside where they'd lain entwined. "Give it to me," he said. "We might need it on the way."

He hoped to hell not, but precautions were necessary. For all he knew, the man who'd shot him might not have been acting alone.

She handed him his weapon. She'd already set the safety, so he jammed it in the waist of his pants.

His radio beeped in, and Jane retrieved it from his pack and handed it to him. He pressed it to his ear and stepped outside, motioning for her to wait inside while he scanned the area for danger.

"Fletch, it's Todd. Jacob's here."

Fletch froze, heart hammering. "I'm here. Over."

"I heard you were shot. Are you okay, man?" Worry sharpened his brother's voice.

"Yeah, Jane Doe removed the bullet and stitched me up."

"Really?"

"Really."

"Where is she?"

"We holed up in a shelter last night, and are about to set out. She's inside waiting for me to give her the all clear." He was just about to tell Jacob about the mass murder theory but Jacob cut him off.

"Good. Let her wait a minute."

Fletch didn't like the raw edge to his brother's voice. "What's going on?"

"Fletch, a woman matching the description of your Jane Doe is wanted for murdering her husband in Asheville." Jacob paused, his breathing strained. "Be careful, man. Her name is Bianca, and, according to the report, she's dangerous."

Chapter Nine

Fletch glanced back at the doorway where Jane stood. She looked pale yet beautiful in the early morning light. Her dark hair hung in waves over her shoulders, her green eyes serious as she searched the area.

Jacob's statement echoed in his ears. *Jane matches the description of a woman wanted for murdering her husband in Asheville. Her name is Bianca, and she's dangerous.*

"Are you sure?" Fletch asked.

"I talked to an officer there myself," Jacob said. "He texted me a picture of the crime scene. It was a bloody mess. Husband, Victor Renard, was shot square between the eyes."

Just like the man Jane had shot.

She had known how to handle the gun. Had made a shot that, for a beginner, was almost impossible. But she'd killed him in self-defense.

That heated kiss taunted him.

Dammit, just when he'd started to trust her...

"There has to be more to the story," he said,

angry with himself for allowing Jane to get under his skin. "When I found her, she was bruised and suffering from a head injury. After we started hiking, we came on another shelter where we found rope and a rag. Jane claims she was tied and gagged and left there."

A heartbeat of silence passed. Jacob cleared his throat. "Could she be lying?"

Jacob scrubbed a hand over his face as memories of another woman lying to him flashed back. Hannah Miller. She'd fooled him with her damsel-in-distress act.

But this was different. Wasn't it? "Her injuries are real and she was almost dead when I found her. Rope burns marked her wrists and ankles. And I saw the gash on the back of her head." He couldn't imagine the wound being self-inflicted.

"What did she tell you about what happened?"

"So far not much. She appears to have amnesia. Could be caused from the head injury or trauma."

Another moment of silence. "Do you believe her?"

"Yeah, I do. Her frustration over her memory loss seems genuine." Fletch paused. "She also mentioned having nightmares where she thinks she might have witnessed a mass murder. Something about a neighborhood barbecue."

Jacob cleared his throat. "Let me dig around some more and see what I can find out on Bianca and her husband. And I'll look into mass murders although nothing about one at a neighborhood barbecue rings a bell."

"Thanks. We're heading out to hike down the mountain now."

Jacob's breath rattled over the line. "Be careful, little brother. And watch your back. If Jane Doe is Bianca Renard and she's on the run from the law, she could turn on you at any minute."

Fletch assured him he'd stay alert for trouble. Although he'd given Jane his gun the night before and she'd done nothing except take care of him.

Which meant her amnesia was real or she was a damn good liar.

Either way, he'd watch her every second.

JANE SENSED SOMETHING different with Fletch as they started down the mountain. Ever since that radio transmission, he'd been quiet and suspicion laced his eyes as if he was scrutinizing her every move.

Finally, a mile down the mountain, she leaned against a tree to catch her breath and confronted him. "What's wrong, Fletch? Do you have information about me?"

Fletch rubbed at his thigh. It was obviously hurting him, but he hadn't complained or allowed it to slow him down. "First, you tell me—have you remembered who you are?"

Jane's pulse hammered at the distrust in his voice. "No, why? Do you know who I am?"

Fletch shrugged. "Jacob received a missing persons report on a woman matching your description."

Jane's breath stalled in her chest. She sensed she wasn't going to like what Fletch had to tell her. "What is my name?"

"He's not a hundred percent sure it's you," Fletch warned. "I couldn't send him pics because there's no phone reception here on this part of the mountain."

Anxiety needled Jane. "Just tell me what he said, Fletch."

Fletch released a weary sigh. "The woman's name is Bianca Renard."

Jane shifted, mentally repeating the name in her head. Bianca... That didn't seem right.

In fact, Jane felt more like her name than Bianca.

Fletch remained silent, studying her with hawklike eyes. "Does the name sound familiar?"

She slowly shook her head. "Not really. What else did he say about this woman?"

Fletch pulled a hand down his chin, drawing her gaze back to his beard-stubbled jaw and those lips that had kissed her. For a moment during the kiss, she'd forgotten she was in danger. She'd felt safe.

She didn't feel safe anymore.

"She was married to a man named Victor."

"Victor?" She tossed that name around just as she had the name Bianca. "You said she was married as in she isn't anymore?"

Fletch gave a small nod. "Victor was murdered, shot to death."

Jane barely stifled a gasp as the image of the man with the tattoo on his arm surfaced. His body flying backward. Blood spewing.

Her hand shaking as she gripped the gun...

She had to swallow twice to make her voice work. "Do they know who killed him?"

Silence stretched long and thick, filled with the threat of an accusation.

"At this point, Bianca is wanted for his murder." Oh, God.

Jane sank down onto the ground and dropped her head into her hands. She didn't remember a wedding or vows or sleeping with this man she'd married.

But she had seen his murder in her mind. Worse, she'd been holding the gun.

FLETCH STUDIED JANE'S reaction for signs she was staging it, but she seemed truly distraught.

"Does any of this sound familiar?" he asked.

She blinked as if needing to focus as she looked up at him. "I had a brief flashback where I saw the man who'd given me the wedding ring being shot," she admitted. "But I'm not sure who shot him."

The old adage "innocent until proven guilty" reverberated in Fletch's head. "Jacob didn't know details, but he's going to dig around and find out more about Bianca and her husband. When we get back to Whistler, hopefully he'll have answers."

Jane nodded, although wariness mixed with worry in her eyes.

"God, Fletch. If I killed my husband," she said, "the man who shot at us might have been a cop."

Fletch considered her theory. "If he was a cop, he would have identified himself as one instead of opening fire and attacking you."

Jane tugged her hat over her ears as a gust of wind blew through. "True."

Fletch searched for an alternative explanation. "If you witnessed a crime, that might explain the reason a hit man would come after you. Someone doesn't want you to talk."

A troubled expression creased her face.

He extended his hand to help her up. "Ready?"

She clasped his hand, their gazes locking. Jacob's warning taunted Fletch. But the woman looking back at him did not look like a cold-blooded killer.

Don't be a fool, another voice inside his head whispered. *Just because she's pretty and in trouble, it doesn't mean you can let down your guard.*

"I appreciate your honesty, Fletch. Thanks for not instantly believing I'm a murderer," Jane said softly.

"Just don't lie to me, Jane. Tell me when you remember something," he said gruffly.

Another gust of wind blew through, and Jane shivered, then released his hand. She brushed snow and debris from the seat of her pants, then took off down the trail.

He was a half mile down when he realized she hadn't responded to his request.

JANE LATCHED ON TO Fletch's theory, mentally trying to fit together the pieces in her mind to create a picture of what had happened.

But there were still too many holes.

As they hiked over brush and along jagged ridges, her boots skidded, and she clawed at tree branches to maintain her balance. Twice she slipped, but Fletch caught her, the tension between them palpable.

Although the theory that she was in danger because she'd witnessed a murder made sense, uncertainty plagued his eyes.

How could she blame him? Doubts filled her at every turn.

Fletch suddenly threw up a hand for her to wait. The sun was warming the frozen ground, slush slowing them as their shoes sank deep into the icy water and mud. A noise from the left startled her, and she realized the sound was the reason Fletch had halted.

A limb snapped off and flew downward, and

she ducked sideways to avoid being hit in the head. Fletch clutched his weapon as he surveyed the area surrounding them.

More noise. Brush rustling. Twigs snapping.

A movement ahead. Then another.

Jane dug her fingernails into her palms as she waited.

Fletch motioned for her to stay where she was, and she flattened herself against the trunk of a tall pine. Snow fluttered from the shivering trees, raining down in a white shower.

Suddenly more movement ahead. She caught sight of reddish brown fur. Two of them.

Wolves.

Fletch motioned for her to be very still, and she was, waiting. At one time red wolves faced extinction, so she didn't condone killing them unless it was for self-preservation. No need to provoke them now.

She and Fletch remained immobile, giving the wolves time to create some distance between them. Finally she released the breath she'd been holding, and she inched up beside Fletch. He rubbed his leg again, and she touched his arm. "Let me check the bandage. It looks like you're bleeding again."

"I'm fine," Fletch said.

"Don't be silly," Jane said. "We need to stop the bleeding and change your dressing."

He made a low sound of frustration, then limped

over to a big rock and sat down. He dropped the pack on the ground, and Jane retrieved the first aid kit. She gently removed the bloody bandage and cleaned the wound. Fletch winced, sweat beading on his forehead. He was obviously hurting but was too proud to ask for help.

"You should have called your team to come for you," Jane admonished while she pressed a blood stopper to the wound.

"In my job, we have to prioritize. Right now other people need help more than I do."

Jane fought a smile at his stubborn independence. "Right." She applied pressure to the wound. Cold air swirled around her as she waited to stop the bleeding.

"You did a nice job stitching me up," he said in a gruff tone.

Jane shrugged. "My first time. At least, I think it was." The empty void in her mind threatened to choke her with despair again.

Fletch squeezed her shoulder. "It'll be all right. We'll uncover the truth about you."

"I hope so." She bit down on her bottom lip. "At the moment, I'm worried about you hiking on that leg."

Fletch shrugged, a twinkle in his eyes. "Don't worry about me. I'm a tough guy."

Tough and sexy. And a real true-life hero.

Tears blurred her vision, but she blinked them

away and made quick work of applying another bandage.

"Thanks," he said as she stowed the emergency kit again.

"You're welcome." She stood and brushed snow from her clothing.

Fletch jammed his gun back in the waistband of his pants and gestured he was ready to proceed. Jane followed his lead, winding down a trail so narrow that she felt as if they were going to slide off the mountain.

They reached another thicket of trees, then stepped through an opening flanked by a cluster of rocks.

Fletch came to a halt again, his hand pressing her behind him. Jane glanced over his shoulder, then gasped.

A man lay in the snow between the boulders, his clothing torn and bloody, his arms and legs bent at odd angles, his eyes staring wide open in death.

Chapter Ten

The sight of the dead man twisted at Fletch's gut. He lay stomach down on the rocks, with his face angled slightly to one side.

On first thought, he wondered if he'd fallen and hit his head. But in light of the fact that someone had tried to kill Jane, suspicions kicked in.

Fletch touched her shoulder. "Stay here. Let me take a look."

Jane's complexion turned pasty white. The man in him wanted to comfort her, but the professional ordered him to do his job.

Take pictures. Report the body. Let the evidence speak for itself.

Considering the circumstances, he had to ask, "Do you recognize this man?"

Jane wrinkled her forehead in thought. "No."

"Let me photograph the scene. Sit down and take a deep breath," he instructed. "I'll be right back."

Fletch retrieved his camera from his pack and captured different angles of the man's body and the surrounding area. Talon marks and his torn clothing indicated he'd been mauled by birds of prey, probably postmortem.

Fletch inched forward, senses honed for trouble as he approached the body. The man had been dressed for the elements, insulated pants, snow boots, flannel shirt, winter coat, gloves and hat, although the hat had come off and lay in the snow.

Definitely a significant amount of blood had pooled beneath the man's face.

Fletch snapped photographs of his clothing, the way his limbs were twisted and distorted, then eased close enough to examine him further.

Wiry, dirty blond hair. Blood matted on the back of his head. A scar on his face that looked old, as if he'd been in a fight with a knife at some point in his life.

Fletch pulled gloves from his pocket and slipped them on, then pushed the man's hair aside. A bullet wound had pierced the back of his skull.

He gently rolled the man's head to one side to assess the gunshot. Blood and brain matter covered the rocks and surrounding area, confirming the man had been shot from behind.

"Fletch?" Jane said in a raw whisper.

"He was murdered, gunshot wound." Fletch turned to gauge her reaction. She instinctively rubbed her fingers across the back of her own head.

"I need to call this in." He retrieved his radio from his pack and connected with the station. "Fletch here. Found a man shot to death. Looks like he's been dead a few hours at least." He gave the coordinates. "Notify Jacob. I'll look for evidence and collect what I find. Send a recovery team when possible."

Fletch ended the call, then combed the area surrounding the rocks for the bullet. A few feet away, he spotted the casing in the midst of a pile of branches. He dug it out, then bagged it and labeled it to give to Jacob for analysis.

If this bullet casing matched the one from the shooter's gun, they could connect the two. He dug into the man's pockets in search of an ID.

A pack of non-menthol cigarettes, gum, mints, a Swiss army knife and a lighter. No ID.

The clean shot to the head suggested the killer was a professional. He'd probably taken the ID.

If this scar-faced man had been killed by a professional, and the professional was the same man who'd shot at Jane, was he a hired hit man?

Which raised another question—why would a professional killer target Jane?

JANE CURLED HER hands into fists. Fletch wanted to protect her by shielding her from the man's body, but she needed to see his face. To see if he triggered a memory.

To know if he was connected to her amnesia.

According to Fletch's brother, she was wanted for murder. What if there was a bounty on her head? This man and the bearded shooter could have been tracking her down to bring her in.

Even so, who killed this man?

She inched closer, scrutinizing his body size. "Let me see his face," she said quietly.

Fletch angled the man's head to the side. Jane swallowed hard as she studied his features. Shaggy, dirty blond hair. A narrow face, long nose, a jagged scar running from his temple down the left side of his cheek.

Her pulse hammered. Something about the man *was* familiar.

"Jane?"

His name teetered on the edge of her tongue.

Fletch hissed between his teeth. "Maybe Jacob or Liam can ID him, then we determine if his death is connected to you."

His calm acceptance helped soothe her anxiety. "Everything just seems random," she said. "I don't understand the timing, much less if the bits and pieces tell the story."

"Close your eyes and try to relax," Fletch murmured. "Take your time and concentrate. Maybe he had something to do with Victor Renard?"

A brief image of her husband's face flashed behind her eyes. Then she was holding a gun. Then…nothing. A big black hole.

She knotted her hands in frustration.

Fletch squeezed her shoulder. "Listen to me. You're making progress. You just need more time."

Maybe so. But everything she remembered became even more disturbing and was filled with death and violence.

FLETCH WAS DAMN tired of playing the guessing game. He couldn't imagine Jane's agitation.

His past was filled with happy memories of family camping trips, holidays, boisterous family dinners and game nights. He held on to those precious memories, to the sound of his father's voice, to the mouthwatering scent of his mother's homemade peach cobbler, to the joy of their laughter as he and his brothers chased each other through the woods.

One trip stood out—it was hot as hell and buggy. After dinner everyone dove into the swimming hole to escape the heat and mosquitos.

Then they'd huddled around the fire and roasted marshmallows.

The holidays were always special, too. Liam loved scary stories, especially at Halloween. Their mother had decorated the house and yard with spiders and ghosts and goblins, while his father made up a spooky story about the house down the street being inhabited by pirate ghosts.

He couldn't imagine losing those memories or living with an empty void in his mind.

Or not having a family.

Yet he'd been so focused on hunting down the arsonist who'd taken his father from them that he hadn't considered having a family of his own. Not until he'd seen Jacob with Cora and her daughter.

The love between his brother and his new wife sparked his own desire to have someone special in his life.

He glanced at Jane's pale face and grimaced. That kiss had been hot.

But she was embroiled in something deep. If Jacob's report was right, she might have murdered her husband. Of course, there could be a plausible reason.

Abuse topped the list. Or self-defense… Perhaps she'd learned something about her husband he didn't want exposed. Perhaps she'd witnessed her husband commit a murder, and he'd wanted to keep her quiet.

Or…perhaps he was grasping because he *wanted* Jane to be innocent.

His radio crackled, and he connected. "Fletch here. Over."

"It's Jacob. Todd sent a message saying you found a body. Do you have a name?"

"No, no ID on him." Fletch explained about the bullet wound to the back of the man's head. "I took pictures and gathered what might be evidence to bring back. I've also requested a recovery team."

"Copy that. I'll make sure the ME and my deputy accompany them."

"Do you want me to stay here and secure the scene until the team arrives?" Fletch asked.

A hesitation on Jacob's part. "No. I want you down here for medical treatment."

"I'm fine," Fletch said. "Jane did a good job of patching me up."

Another heartbeat of silence. "Speaking of Jane, did you ask her about Bianca and Victor Renard?"

Fletch angled himself away from Jane so she couldn't hear his conversation.

She kept looking at the dead man as if he held the secrets to her past.

"Yes, but the names don't ring a bell. Did you find out more about the Renards?"

"According to my source, Bianca worked as an interior designer with her real estate husband. He owned his own company that was worth a few million. Bianca staged new homes for him as well as handling her own client list.

"The couple just moved to Asheville. So far, I haven't located any family or friends to verify this information, but I'm working on it."

"Financial trouble?" Fletch asked.

"I'm just getting started. I'll have one of our analysts dig into their financials to see if there's anything fishy."

"Something worth murdering for."

"Yeah. I'll keep you posted." Jacob paused. "And Fletch?"

"Yeah?"

"Be careful, man. Looks can be deceiving. This woman might be serious trouble."

Hannah had certainly deceived him. She'd pretended to love him, but in the end, she'd wanted money and nice things, not a mountain man who lived his days in the woods.

Fletch ended the connection and walked back over to Jane. She looked at him expectantly. "That was Jacob."

Her sharp intake of breath punctuated the air between them. "What did he say?"

Fletch shrugged. For some reason, he couldn't reconcile the information Jacob had shared with Jane's behavior.

"Tell me what you know, Fletch."

The need in her voice roused his protective instincts again. But sharing might trigger her lost memories to resurface.

So he relayed Jacob's statement. "Does any of that ring a bell?"

Jane pursed her lips. "He said I'm an interior designer?"

He nodded. "Your husband Victor was a big wheel in real estate, worth millions."

She furrowed her brows. "In my dreams, I was at a neighborhood cookout. It was in the suburbs somewhere. And it seemed…normal." She worried her bottom lip with her teeth. "If I decorated houses, why can't I recall that? And for some reason, I can't imagine I had money like that."

"You may be repressing the memories because someone you loved hurt you. Have you considered the fact that it was your husband?"

"I HAVE." SHE'D OBVIOUSLY seen something that had been so horrible she didn't want to remember it.

But she couldn't move on with her future until she did.

The wind picked up again, howling off the mountain. Snow was starting to melt quickly, tree limbs cracking and breaking off.

She glanced back at the dead man, willing him to talk to her.

"We'd better get going," Fletch said. "I'd like for us to make it down the mountain before dark tonight."

Jane's stomach churned as they left the body lying on the rocks and began to hike again. Fletch adjusted his pack to alleviate extra weight on his injured leg, then led her down another path.

After two more miles, everything looked the same to her. Endless miles of forest, trees so thick they practically hugged each other and let in very little light. A gray fog covered the sky, adding to the dismal feel.

She was grateful for Fletch's experience on

the trail or she would have been lost. The frozen ground became slushy and slippery, her boots sinking into freezing water that went all the way through to her socked feet. The trees swayed in the wind, and melting snow began running downhill like a river.

Another mile, and suddenly a loud noise sounded. Fletch went still, and cocked his head to listen. A shudder coursed through Jane as a rumbling noise boomeranged off the mountain. Fletch pivoted, and eyes widening, grabbed her hand.

"Avalanche," he shouted. "Hurry. Let's go."

Jane spotted the mounds of snow beginning to barrel down the mountain toward them.

She and Fletch tried to outrun it, but the landslide was so fast and sudden that the force of it nearly knocked her down. Fletch clutched her hand to steady her and pulled her to the right.

"Cave. Inside," he shouted.

She ducked her head as he yanked her into the opening. Snow and debris rained down in a thunderous roar, rocks and ice tumbling.

A second later, the avalanche dumped mounds of snow and ice in front of the door, blocking their exit.

Jane's lungs squeezed for air. They were trapped.

Chapter Eleven

Dammit to hell and back. How much more could go wrong on this trek?

Fletch had undertaken countless missions, some involving major emergencies, some where they recovered bodies instead of rescuing individuals.

But never one where he was ambushed by a shooter and then found a man murdered. And now, on top of the blizzard, a freak avalanche.

"Jane, are you hurt?" He quickly glanced at her as he urged her away from the cave entrance.

"I'm okay," she said. "But what caused that?"

Fletch sank back on his heels, his eyes adjusting to the dimly lit interior of the cave. Stone walls, dirt floor and wooden braces indicated it had once been an active mine. "Happens sometimes after a big snowstorm when the weather changes abruptly."

Jane fingered her tangled hair from her cheek. "It sounded like an explosion, like dynamite exploding."

He'd thought the same thing.

Which meant the avalanche might not have been caused by nature, but it could have been intentional.

Someone else after Jane? Or Bianca, if that was her name? He still couldn't reconcile the name Bianca or her job as an interior designer with the skilled fighter and shooter he'd witnessed.

Although it was possible she'd taken a self-defense class as she'd suggested. God knows, women needed to these days. There were too many damn predators on the streets.

"Fletch, do you think someone set off dynamite?"

Fletch chewed the inside of his cheek. He didn't want to alarm her when he had no answer, just suspicions. "I don't know. We can't jump to conclusions, Jane. Sometimes the sound of ice breaking and the force of the wind sound like an explosion. Remember my teammate said they were rescuing people from another avalanche."

Jane propped herself against the wall of the cave, eyes flickering with fear as she glanced at the doorway. "What do we do now?"

"Don't panic." Fletch removed his radio from his pack and tried to connect, but static rattled in the air. Dammit. "I gave Jacob the coordinates for the dead man we found on the rocks. It's not far from here. When a team comes to recover his body, they'll find us."

"But they don't even know we're missing."

Fletch pasted on an encouraging smile. "My brother was expecting us to be down the mountain in a couple of hours. When we don't show, he'll try to make contact. If he can't get through, he'll organize a search party to look for us."

Jane released a wary sigh. "How can you be so confident?"

"I trust my brothers," he said. "They'll look for us. And Jacob is logical. He knows the path I'd travel from those rocks, and he'll follow it. It's only a matter of time."

A frown puckered the skin between Jane's eyes. "It must be nice to be so close to your family, to know that your brothers are there for you no matter what."

A wealth of sadness weighted her words, and Fletch tilted her chin up with his thumb and looked into her eyes. "You're going to remember, Jane, and whatever happened, you'll get through it. You might even have someone in your life looking for you. Another family member. A friend. Someone who loves you."

Emotions clouded her eyes. "I don't know, Fletch. I…feel like I'm alone, that I have been for a long time. That I don't have anybody."

Jacob's warning echoed in Fletch's mind. But he had to trust his gut instincts instead. And they were screaming at him that Jane was an innocent victim who needed understanding and protection.

Unable to resist, he raked debris from the avalanche from her hair, then drew her to him and kissed her.

THE AFFECTION IN Fletch's voice when he'd spoken about his family made Jane long for that kind of closeness with someone.

Made her want a family that she could count on, someone to love.

Fletch's lips closed over hers, moving gently with a mixture of erotic teasing and tenderness. The sincerity in his eyes just before he'd kissed her moved something deep inside her.

She lifted one hand and pressed it against his jaw, her senses heightened by the intimacy of the dark, cold interior. The fear and panic that had nearly immobilized her earlier dissipated as he deepened the kiss and threaded his fingers through her hair.

He angled his head, drew closer and teased her lips apart with his tongue. Desire surged through her.

Heart hammering, she met his tongue thrust for thrust. He trailed one hand down her shoulder to pull her against him. Her breasts tingled at the feel of his hard, muscular chest.

Craving more, Jane stroked his back and made a low sound of need in her throat. Fletch tore his lips from hers, his breathing erratic. Passion glazed his dark chocolate eyes, hunger flaring between them.

He was asking for permission.

She obliged and pulled him back to her, then unbuttoned the top button of his flannel shirt. His breath rushed out, and he lowered his head and dropped kisses along her throat then lower to the sensitive skin between her breasts. With a low groan, he peeled back her shirt and tasted her skin.

A frenzy of hunger seized them, and their movements became more frantic. He kissed her again, deep and long and greedily, then suckled at her neck until she unfastened the buttons on his shirt and pushed the fabric off his broad shoulders. He tossed the garment aside, then tugged his T-shirt over his head, exposing bare flesh, corded muscles and a dark sprinkling of hair that trailed from his chest down to the waistband of his pants.

Warmth pooled in her body, and an ache built, which made her run her hands over his bare skin. Heat tingled through her at his sharp intake of breath.

"Jane?"

"Yes," she said in a ragged whisper. Passion and need overcame reason, and she leaned forward and pressed kisses along his chest.

Fletch groaned, then pushed her onto her back and dove in for another long, sensual kiss. His hard length pressed into the V of her thighs, stroking her through her pants, and she lifted her hips as erotic sensations pummeled her.

Fletch dipped his head and nibbled at the sensitive skin between her breasts, then suckled her through the thin lace of her bra. Jane whispered his name and clung to him, welcoming the cool brush of air as he unfastened the front clasp of her bra, exposing her breasts. Her nipples stiffened to peaks, begging for his touch.

He tugged one into his mouth and suckled her, driving her mad with desire. She raked her nails over his back, urging him on, and parted her legs in invitation.

He moved to her other breast, giving it the same loving attention, and she tugged at his belt. He moved lower, pulling at her pants, and she lifted her hips to give him access.

He gazed at her with such hunger that her body tingled with need. He paused, eyes flaring with lust as he traced a finger along the edge of her black lace panties.

Hungry for more, for all of him, she freed his belt then tossed it aside. Then she pushed at his pants. But the sight of his bandage made her pause.

"Fletch?"

His body braced on his elbows, he looked down into her face. "Jane…we shouldn't."

Hurt battled with the realization that he was right.

"I'm sorry." He moved off her and handed her clothing to her, then snatched his and turned his back to her.

She stared at the beautiful hard planes of his back and longed to draw him back to her and finish what they'd begun.

But the stiff set of his shoulders and his apology felt like a rejection. She wouldn't beg him to make love to her.

But he *had* seemed to want her.

Why had he suddenly changed his mind?

FLETCH QUICKLY BUTTONED his shirt, silently berating himself for allowing things to go so far.

He knew damn well better than to get personally involved with Jane. She had amnesia and was vulnerable. What the hell was wrong with him?

He'd never had trouble keeping it in his pants before.

But he'd never felt so drawn to anyone the way he felt drawn to Jane.

The fear and loneliness in her eyes completely shredded his common sense and willpower.

But if she was an interior designer and came from money, she might want to return to that world. Just as Hannah had.

That life was the polar opposite of his. One he would never fit into.

Needing to regain his composure, he forced himself not to look at her. Instead he tried the radio, but once again, only static crackled off the rocky mine walls. Deciding to hunt for another way out, he told Jane to stay put and he carried his flashlight to look around.

Damp moss clung to the stone walls, the ground solid dirt. He found an area where he could stand, then noticed there was an opening leading to another area, so he followed it. He had to crouch low to keep from hitting his head in several places. Water trickled down the sides of the interior, and he rounded a curve. He wove through a few other turns and followed the tunnel hoping to find an exit, but the tunnel ended with a hard wall.

Damn.

Irritated, he turned and started back toward Jane.

Breathing out, he shined the light around, his pulse clamoring when he spotted another clearing to the right. He inched through the narrow path to it, and found an old glove on the ground.

There were also bits of wrappers from dried food packs and boot prints. He knelt to examine them and determined they were large, probably a man's. From his vantage, he noticed a small spiral notepad on the ground wedged between some rocks.

With gloved hands, he tugged it free and

opened it to examine the pages. A crudely drawn map of the trail. He flipped a page and paused, his heart hammering.

An article about the Whistler Hospital fire was folded and pressed between the pages.

The newspaper clipping could mean nothing. But for five years, he'd wondered if the person who'd set that fire was hiding out in these woods. What if he was right?

What if that man had been staying in this cave?

Adrenaline spiked his blood, and he ran back through the cave to retrieve his camera and bags for the evidence he'd discovered. Jane was sitting with her knees up, arms around them, staring at the doorway, her expression a mask of worry.

"I found some things in the back of the cave," he said. "I need to collect them to give to Jacob."

Jane glanced at him. "Do you think they belong to the dead man we found on the rocks?"

Fletch shrugged. "It's possible." Although he'd rather believe they belonged to the arsonist. Then he might catch a break and give Jacob and Liam a lead.

"I'll be right back."

He didn't wait for her to comment. He hurried through the tunnels and collected the glove and notebook.

Excited at the prospect of finally catching the bastard who killed his father, he carried the evidence back to where Jane waited and stowed it in his pack.

He was anxious to give them to Jacob for processing.

Jane looked ashen-faced in the dim light, and he fought the urge to return to her and comfort her. If he touched her again, he might not be able to stop himself from making love to her.

Instead he retrieved a tool from his pack and began to chisel at the fallen snow and ice trapping them inside.

JANE SENSED AN urgency about Fletch's rush to dig them an escape hole. "What did you find in the cave?"

Fletch sat back on his haunches. "A glove and a notebook indicating someone had been staying here. An article about the fire was tucked inside the book."

Hope tinged his voice. "Maybe the crime lab can lift prints from the items," Fletch said. "If they belong to the person who set the fire, we can identify him. If not, maybe they belong to someone with helpful information."

She admired his determination. Fletch was obviously not the kind of man who gave up on a cause.

"If he is the person who cost all those lives, he should pay," Jane said and meant it.

His gaze locked with hers, his dark eyes probing. The fact that she was wanted for murder taunted her.

The air suddenly became harder to breathe. She had to look away from Fletch for fear he'd see the self-doubts plaguing her.

Desperate for the truth, she crawled over to him. "If you have another tool, I'll help."

"I've got it," he said.

She rolled her eyes at his macho tone. "I may have amnesia but I'm not helpless, Fletch." She scanned the interior of the cave and found a jagged rock on the ground, so she snatched it.

Then she began to hack away at the top edge of the opening. Fletch didn't comment. He chiseled away alongside her.

"Tell me more about your family," Jane urged as they worked.

Fletch sighed. "My mother was a great cook," he said. "She took pride in feeding her boys. She made the best pot roast in the state, and her peach cobbler was to die for. She loved big Sunday dinners and would have really enjoyed having grandkids." A smile tugged at the corners of his mouth. "She volunteered with a children's charity and devoted her free time to help provide underprivileged children with meals at school and during summer break."

"She sounds like a great lady," Jane said.

"She was. We lost her not long after we lost Dad. I think she died of heartbreak." Sadness filled his voice. "What do you recall about your mother?"

Jane bit down on her lip. She and her father shared the crosswords. But her mother... "Not that much," she said. "I think she was social and liked to entertain." And she sensed she was the opposite. Not a girlie girl as her mother wanted. "In one of my dreams, I saw law books on my father's desk. I think he might have been a lawyer. Maybe a judge."

Fletch jabbed the tool in the ice again. "Do you think their murder had something to do with his job? That it wasn't a random home invasion?"

Jane paused in her chiseling. "I...don't remember, but I suppose it's possible."

Fletch rubbed her shoulder. "Things are starting to come back to you, Jane. When we get home, maybe everything will come back."

All the more reason to keep chiseling.

Jane turned back to work, and so did Fletch. They chipped away ice and snow, digging to create an opening, but after an hour they'd barely made a dent. Fletch refused to give up, though. He continued until a sliver of light and air appeared.

But a noise outside rumbled, then suddenly rocks and dirt inside the cave began to tumble down. Jane screamed. The ceiling was caving in!

Fletch grabbed her hand. "Come on, get away from that side!"

They crawled toward the tunnel leading to the back, then another thunderous noise and rocks and dirt started raining down.

Fletch threw himself on top of her and covered her with his body to protect her as the deluge pummeled them.

Chapter Twelve

Rocks thundered to the ground, the crashing sound reverberating off the cave walls. Jane coughed as dust flew into her face, but she lay still, praying the entire cave didn't crumble on top of them.

She didn't want to die here buried in rubble without clearing her name. Or even knowing who she was.

Slowly, the downfall slowed, the ping of stones and debris lessening. Fletch slowly lifted himself off her. "Are you okay, Jane?"

She nodded, brushing dirt from her mouth as she raised her head and peered toward the cave entrance. The opening was completely blocked with inches of dirt and rocks. "I am. Are you?"

"Yeah." He swore beneath his breath as he surveyed the damage.

Panic clawed at Jane. "We're really trapped now, Fletch."

Fletch clasped her hand and squeezed it. "For now, maybe. But my team will find us."

She wished she had his confidence. But she was unable to hide her fear. She might not know much about herself, but she didn't like small spaces.

He gently brushed dirt from her cheek. "Remember what I said before. My brothers will look for me and so will my team. The cave is near where we found that man's body. Once they see the avalanche, they'll launch a search."

Jane desperately wanted to believe him. The thought of suffocating in the darkness terrified her.

"Come on," Fletch said softly. "Let's move away from the mess. The air will be better back there."

She clutched his hand. "But what if someone comes? We won't be able to hear them."

Fletch released a breath. "We won't go far, just far enough to breathe better."

She relented and realized he was right. The air felt cooler, clearer, her breathing more steady as they crawled to a wider section of the cave. Fletch leaned against the wall beside her, his expression calm, although worry shadowed his eyes.

FLETCH REINED IN his mounting anxiety. He wanted to start digging them out again, but the explosion had damaged the structural foundation of the cave, and he didn't trust that the whole damn place wouldn't collapse on top of them.

"What if the man who tried to kill me set off that explosion to make sure we didn't survive?"

Compassion for Jane replaced his need to keep his distance. "It's possible, I suppose. But you shot him when he ambushed us."

"He could have had an accomplice who's still out there."

"Then who is the dead man on the rocks?"

Jane pinched the bridge of her nose. "I wish I knew."

Fletch mentally sorted through the possibilities. "At this point, we can only speculate. Let's go over what we know so far."

Jane nodded. "I remember being attacked by a man, tied and gagged in that cave. I tried to escape and he found me and knocked me unconscious and left me in the blizzard to die."

"Man number one—attacker."

"I also remember a man with a wolf tattoo on his arm. He put the wedding ring on my finger."

"Man number two is the husband."

Jane shrugged. "Then there was the bearded man who shot at us. The one I killed."

"In self-defense," Fletch reminded her. "So the bearded shooter was man number three."

"And now the dead man with the scar on his face, who we found on the rocks," Jane added. "That makes four."

"Which means the bearded shooter and the scar-faced dead man may or may not have been your attacker. It's possible they're connected, that one or more of them were being paid to find you."

Jane dropped her head in her hands and groaned. "And there's the question—why do they want me dead?"

Fletch rubbed the back of her neck. "I know it's disconcerting, Jane. But we will solve this mystery."

Jane looked up at him with such helplessness that he forgot his reservations. He pulled her into his arms and stroked her back. "Just hang in there."

She tilted her head to search his face. "But what if I'm guilty of killing my husband like your brother suggested?"

"If you did, then there must have been a good reason," Fletch assured her.

PANIC NEEDLED JANE, and she and Fletch fell into an awkward silence. She prayed he was right about her. She didn't want to escape this cave only to be locked in a cell the rest of her life.

As the hours dragged by, the interior of the cave grew smaller and darker. Her anxiety intensified with every passing minute. She didn't know if the air was harder to breathe because it was running out, or if the fear squeezing at her lungs was making her paranoid.

Eventually fatigue claimed her, and she curled against Fletch. He wrapped his arm around her, stroked her back again, and she drifted to sleep. Occasionally when she stirred, she heard the soft sound of Fletch's breathing.

Comforted by his presence, she closed her eyes and sleep claimed her again. But even in sleep, the nightmares returned to haunt her.

The blood...her parents' faces...her husband's tattoo, his body flying backward, the gun clenched in her hand...

Then she was running for her life. Someone was behind her. She felt his breath, heard his hiss as he closed in on her. Then his hands snatching her, a blow to the head...and she was spinning and falling into the darkness.

Then gunfire. She gasped for breath. She was trapped in a cave. The air was gone. She was dying...

She jerked awake at the same time Fletch did. A noise somewhere. Fletch released her and crawled nearer the cave exit. Jane joined him, perched on her knees, listening.

There it was again. A low noise… Voices.

Hope bloomed in her chest. Fletch snatched his radio and attempted to make contact again, but failed. Voices echoed again.

"Hello?" he shouted. "We're in here!"

She and Fletch both began to yell, shouting over and over until she heard a chipping sound. Then a man's voice alerting them they were there to help.

Someone was out there! They were going to be rescued!

Tears of relief blurred her vision. Several seconds passed. A hacking sound. A ping. Voices again.

Seconds bled into agonizing minutes. Finally the debris and snow and ice began to melt away with the rescue workers' efforts. A small hole appeared, enough to allow light and air to flow in.

Jane almost sobbed with relief.

"Fletch?"

This time the voice was loud, distinguishable.

Fletch raised his voice, "Todd, we're in here!"

"We'll have you out soon. Back away from the opening."

"Copy that."

Fletch clutched Jane's hand, and they crawled away from the exit and leaned against the back wall. Dust floated through the air, making it difficult to breathe again, and Jane covered her mouth with her hand to keep from inhaling it.

She thought the workers would never break through, but finally they cleared a hole large enough for them to slip through.

"You go first," Fletch told Jane. "I'll follow."

Jane sucked in a breath, then straightened her arms and dove through the clearing as if she was diving into a swimming pool. Two men grabbed her arms and helped pull her to the other side where she collapsed, coughing and fighting for breath.

FLETCH WAS NEVER so happy to see his buddies in all his life. Not that he'd lied to Jane. He trusted them with his life.

But they'd survived one shooter and if that explosion had been meant to trap or kill them, he needed backup.

Todd had brought a medical team, and they rushed toward Jane. Todd and Jacob approached him.

"You okay, Fletch?" Todd asked.

He nodded. "Thanks," Fletch said. "I knew my team would find us."

Todd rubbed a hand down his chin. "You helped by giving Jacob your coordinates for that body on the rocks."

"I sent my deputy with a team to recover the corpse, and another team has gone out to collect the body of the man who shot you," Jacob interjected. "Now you need to go to the hospital."

Fletch offered Jacob an encouraging look to reassure him he was okay. Knowing the trauma he and his brothers had suffered when they lost their parents, he hated scaring them.

Jacob gestured for the medics to examine him anyway.

"I'm fine," Fletch protested. "Jane needs medical attention. She sustained a head injury and is still suffering from amnesia."

"You have a damn gunshot wound, brother," Jacob said. "You're going to the hospital, too."

"That's ridiculous." Fletch pushed up to stand, but his leg buckled slightly.

"See?" Jacob said with enough emotion that Fletch relented.

"All right, I'll ride with Jane in the ambulance and we'll both get checked out."

"Fletch," Jacob said in a gruff voice. "What the hell happened between you two?"

A lot. "Nothing," Fletch muttered. "But she seriously needs medical attention. Someone who can help her recover her memory."

"We'll see she gets it," Jacob assured him. "But don't forget—if she's Bianca Renard, she's wanted for murder."

Fletch glared at Jacob. "So you told me. But nothing I've seen about Jane suggests she's a cold-blooded killer."

A gust of wind picked up, scattering snow and debris and sending melting ice from the trees down in a shower.

"You seem defensive of her," Jacob muttered, his voice distressed.

"Because I think she's a victim," Fletch said.

"Thanks, Fletch, but I can stand up for myself." Jane's voice echoed from behind him, and he realized she'd broken away from the medic.

Fletch stepped closer to Jane, his protective instincts surging to life. "Jane, this is my brother Jacob, the sheriff of Whistler."

Jane swayed slightly. "I haven't lied to your brother, Sheriff."

Anger, subtle but real, flickered in Jacob's eyes.

"Listen to me," Jacob said to Jane. "You and Fletch are both going to the hospital for tests and exams. Then you have to answer some questions."

Jane lifted her chin in a show of defiance, or bravado. Fletch wasn't sure which. "I can't tell you what I don't know. But I'll be interested to see what you've uncovered about me."

Jacob and Jane locked horns in a stare down that would have made some men weak in the knees. But Jane stood her ground as if she had her feet back, as if she intended to tackle her problems head-on.

Fletch admired her courage.

He just hoped to hell she got the answers she wanted.

Jacob addressed the medics. "I want her carried down on a stretcher and secured in the ambulance. I'll ride with her and my brother to the hospital."

Jane's mouth twisted with irritation, but she lifted her chin again. "Does that mean I'm under arrest, Sheriff?"

Chapter Thirteen

Fletch studied his brother's body language, but as always Jacob remained calm and cool. Professional.

"Not at the moment, but you are a person of interest. First we verify your identity, then we'll go from there."

Jacob turned to Fletch. "You have evidence for me?"

Fletch jammed his hands in his jacket pocket. "In my pack. I labeled each item and where I found it. There are pictures on my camera, too."

Jacob patted Fletch's back. "Thanks, man. You did good work out there."

A rescue worker helped Jane onto a stretcher, and Fletch angled his head toward Jacob. "I really don't think she remembers, Jacob. And for what it's worth, nothing about her fits with your description of Bianca."

"Liam is digging for more information," Jacob said. "Let the doctor examine her, and I'll send the evidence you found to the lab."

"Good. There's something else. I think the avalanche that caused us to be trapped may have been set intentionally. We were close to digging our way out when there was another explosion. It sounded like dynamite."

"Damn." Jacob lifted a hand to shield his eyes from the blinding morning sun flickering off the white snowy hills.

"I'll send a crime team to search for explosives." He scanned the ridges above them. "Did you see anyone suspicious before the avalanche started?"

"Not really," Fletch said. "Maybe a shadow in the woods."

"Fletch," Jacob said in a low voice. "Be honest. Do you have any idea what's really going on here?"

Fletch's first instinct was to deny that Jane might be complicit in a crime.

But he had to know the truth.

"I have a couple of theories, but they're only that." A gust of wind sent another deluge of snow and ice on them. "Can we discuss it once we get down from the mountain?"

Jacob studied him for a minute. "Sure." He planted a hand on Fletch's chest. "But you are going to the hospital and having that leg looked at. Now get on the stretcher, too."

Fletch shook his head. "No way. I hiked in. I'm hiking out."

Jacob's eyes darkened. "You don't have to prove you're macho, brother."

Fletch laughed. "I'm not. But I refuse to make my men carry a perfectly healthy, strong man down the mountain."

Jacob muttered a sarcastic remark, and Fletch chuckled.

Seconds later the team geared up, and they began the trek down. Jane looked worried as they descended the mountain. Fletch gave her an encouraging look, but he kept his senses peeled for trouble in case another shooter was hiding along the way, waiting to ambush them.

JANE GRITTED HER teeth as the rescue team carried her down the mountain. She might not remember her name or the details of her past, but she instinctively knew she wasn't helpless.

She took care of herself and had been doing so for a long time.

As much as she'd been afraid of dying in that cave, she missed the intimacy she'd shared with Fletch. Being alone with him gave her a sense of safety.

Now she felt his brother's eyes scrutinizing her as if he feared she had sinister intentions toward Fletch.

By the time they reached the bottom of the mountain, she'd worn herself out with questions and doubt. How could she blame Fletch for pulling away when her life was a mystery? Worse, when she was wanted for murdering her own husband?

And his brother… Jacob probably thought she was some kind of Black Widow.

The medics loaded her into the back of an ambulance. Fletch stood with them while Jacob and the rescue team spoke in hushed tones, their heads bunched in conversation. The wind drowned out the sound of their voices, leaving her in the dark.

One of the medics radioed the hospital to report her condition, then Fletch joined her in the back of the ambulance.

His brother Jacob shot her a disapproving look as if he suspected she'd seduced his brother into believing her lies. "I'll be right behind the ambulance."

She reined in her temper and said nothing. If she reacted like a hothead or defended herself, she'd only appear more guilty.

At least he hadn't handcuffed her. But she sensed that was coming. Unless she remembered something in her defense.

The ride to the hospital was steeped in silence, the icy sludge on the ground creating a hazard on the road and slowing the ambulance. When they arrived at the emergency entrance, she and Fletch were wheeled into different exam rooms.

The staff immediately checked her vitals and drew blood for lab work, then encouraged her to submit to a rape exam, although she insisted she hadn't been sexually violated. Still, she understood tests were necessary, and as humiliating as it was, she did want to know who'd hurt her. If she'd had sex before she'd been abandoned in the woods, she wanted to know with whom. And if it was consensual.

A CAT scan came next and then an MRI, after which she was moved to a room. There they hooked her up with an IV to hydrate her, and brought her some warm broth.

It seemed like hours later when the doctor finally appeared. He asked her dozens of questions about herself that she couldn't answer. She struggled to tap into that empty well where her past lay, but failed. No, she didn't remember her birthday or where she'd been born. Or if she had a dog or a cat. Or what her favorite color or song was.

Or how long she'd been married...

"The CAT scan was relatively normal," he reported. "There is some slight swelling around your brain, caused from head trauma. That could account for the amnesia you're experiencing."

"And if it's not the swelling?"

"Physical and/or emotional trauma can cause memory loss. Sometimes we repress memories as a way to protect ourselves."

Except not knowing the truth was putting her in more danger.

"Most likely, with rest and time to heal, your memories will return on their own."

"And if they don't?" Jane asked.

"If you want to speak to a therapist, we can arrange that. There are also alternative treatments, more extensive kinds of psychotherapy, hypnosis, etcetera," he said. "But I don't think we need to go there quite yet."

Of course he didn't. But he wasn't accused of murder.

IMPATIENCE NAGGED AT Fletch as the doctor examined his bullet wound.

"It actually looks good," the doctor said. "You said the woman they brought in removed the bullet and stitched you up?"

"That's right," Fletch replied. And he was anxious to see her again.

"She probably saved you from infection by acting so quickly," the doctor said. "We'll clean your incision and redress it, then you're good to go."

"Thanks." A nurse stepped in and changed the dressing, then Jacob entered the room.

"I'm done," Fletch said as he slid from the exam table. "How's Jane?"

"The doctor wants to keep her overnight for observation. She was dehydrated. He thinks rest may help with the swelling in her brain and the amnesia."

"Did you question her?" Fletch asked.

Jacob grimaced. "Not yet. But I want someone watching her room tonight in case she tries to escape."

Irritation thrummed through Fletch. "No need. I'll stand watch."

Jacob raised his brows. "You were shot, little brother. You need to rest yourself. You probably haven't had a decent meal since you left the bar the other night."

"I'm fine," Fletch insisted. "Besides, Jane trusts me. So if she's going to talk, she might open up to me."

Jacob looked as if he wanted to argue, but finally gave a small nod. "True. But the doc gave her something to help her sleep. She's out for the night now, so I'll stay awhile. Go home, shower and sleep, eat something, then come back in the morning when she wakes up."

Fletch hesitated. But his brother was right. He'd be more clearheaded if he caught some z's. And he needed a shower badly. "All right. But if she wakes, call me."

"Will do. Meanwhile, I need to take Jane's prints and plug them into the system. That will tell us who she is."

Fletch understood Jacob had a job to do. He just hoped to hell that learning Jane's identity would save her, not land her in jail.

THE NEXT MORNING Jane was more rested and less achy. The nurse gave her toiletries for a shower, which made her feel like a new woman.

Jacob's wife sent clean clothes, jeans and a soft blue sweater that were comfortable and warm. A hot breakfast also improved her mood.

Although the grim look in Fletch's eyes when he entered the room with his brother brought reality back fast.

Fletch's gaze skated over her, and for just a moment, she sensed the strong connection they'd shared in the wilderness. A sensual awareness that tempted her to hide in his arms where she'd be safe forever.

This morning he looked sexy in jeans and a denim shirt that accentuated his tanned skin. He'd shaved and she missed the rugged stubble. But the heat in his eyes simmered like the embers of a fire. For a brief second, she wished they'd made love so she could have that memory to keep with her forever.

Then his gaze turned hooded, and an awkwardness settled in the room. "How do you feel this morning?" Fletch asked.

Jane shrugged. "Better. At least clean and fed."

He gave a small smile. "Yeah, me, too."

Jacob cleared his throat. "Has the doctor seen you this morning?"

Jane lifted her chin. "He said I'm clear to go. I'm waiting on the nurse to bring discharge papers."

"What was his opinion regarding the amnesia?" Fletch asked.

Jane pulled a card from the pocket of the jeans. "He gave me a referral to a therapist who might help. She specializes in memory recovery."

"That sounds promising," Fletch said.

Jane exhaled. "I'm supposed to call and set up an appointment." She glanced at Jacob. "That is, if I'm free to do that."

Jacob gave her a flat look. "Last night Officer Clemmens contacted me again. He's the officer who contacted me with the initial report about you. He sent a photograph and confirmation of your identity." Jacob shifted. "Bianca Renard, you are under arrest for the murder of Victor Renard. You have the right to remain silent…"

Knots curled in Jane's gut as he Mirandized her. She'd known this moment might arrive, but being treated like a criminal was humiliating.

"I'm sorry, Jane," Fletch said.

Jane lifted her chin. "I guess it's time I face the truth." Even if she didn't like what she learned about herself.

The nurse poked her head inside, and Jane waved her in. She signed the discharge papers, and was forced to ride to the exit in a wheelchair where the sheriff's car waited.

At least he didn't handcuff her. But the moment the police car door shut, she felt trapped again. She had fought for her life in the woods.

Now she had to fight again.

FLETCH FOLLOWED JACOB to the police station in Whistler, battling anger at the fact that his brother had just arrested Jane. Why he should care so much about a woman he'd known such a short time, and one he knew virtually nothing about, he didn't know.

But he did care, dammit. And he didn't want to see her locked away.

What if she is a murderer?

No…if she *had* killed her husband, there was a reason. A damn good one. He felt it in his soul.

Although he'd been wrong about another woman once. Hannah. She was beautiful and blonde and had the face and voice of an angel.

Too bad she'd possessed the soul of the devil.

Jane sat stone-still as Jacob drove. Fletch admired her steely determination to maintain her composure.

He understood Jacob had to do his job, and couldn't ignore the fact that Jane was wanted in another jurisdiction for murder. If he let her go, the people of Whistler would never trust him to protect them.

Still, Fletch didn't like it one damn bit.

He arrived at the station behind Jacob, his pulse hammering as Jacob opened the back door to his car and helped Jane out.

The hair on the back of his neck prickled. Someone had tried to kill Jane in the woods.

Maybe they still wanted her dead.

As she climbed from the car, he searched the alley by the station and the parking lot for a shooter waiting to ambush.

Chapter Fourteen

A new layer of humiliation washed over Jane as Sheriff Maverick—she couldn't call him Jacob when he was arresting her—fingerprinted her and swabbed her mouth for DNA. A mug shot photo came next.

He escorted her to a small room off the hallway behind the front office. Interrogation Room 1. She was surprised the small town needed more than one, and would have expected crime to be minimal in Whistler.

Then again, the town was so close to the Appalachian Trail that it might attract criminals who wanted to hide out from the law.

She sank into the hard metal chair in front of a wooden table that was bolted to the floor. The sheriff's boots clicked on the wood slats as he crossed to the other side, claimed a seat and placed a manila envelope on the table.

He and Fletch looked like brothers, although their eyes were different and Fletch's hair was longer and shaggy-looking. Fletch also possessed a sexy rawness that made her stomach flutter where Jacob seemed closed off.

Part of his job. He was here to question her, wrangle a confession from her, send her to prison for murder. Not be her friend.

The stain from the fingerprint ink mocked her, and déjà vu struck her. Something about the room, the table, the situation seemed familiar, as if she'd sat at a table like this before. Had she been arrested in the past?

The sheriff pushed a bottle of water in front of her. "The doctor said to stay hydrated."

A sarcastic chuckle rumbled from her. "You're concerned about my health?"

The man's eyes turned stony. "Listen, Jane or Bianca, whatever your name is. I'm aware my brother thinks you're innocent, and I'm not here to railroad you into jail for a crime you didn't commit. But we have to talk."

Jane bit her lip. He was right.

"Let's start with what happened to you. How you ended up on the trail where Fletch found you."

Jane inhaled a deep breath and relayed what little she remembered.

The sheriff studied her, his expression neutral. "So you remember seeing the man you believe to be your husband fall to his death. Then the next thing you remember is running from a man in the woods?"

Jane nodded, straining to recall more details, but the effort was futile and made her head throb.

"What do you remember about the man chasing you? Body size? Height? Color of hair?"

She pinched the bridge of her nose. "He was tall, I think, taller than me. He approached me from behind, so I didn't see his face." She traced her fingers over the back of her head. "He hit me and knocked me out."

Jacob continued, "Then he tied you up and left you in a cave?"

Jane pursed her lips. "I think so, although I just vaguely recall being dragged through the snow there, then I passed out. When I came to, I untied myself and was escaping when he caught me again."

The sheriff folded his arms. "Do you think he was the man you shot?"

Jane released a weary breath. "I honestly don't know. Have you identified him?"

"Not yet. The rescue team recovered his body, and he's on the way to the morgue. So is the other dead man you guys found on those rocks."

She shifted. "I have no idea who he was, either. Although something about him seemed familiar."

"Interesting." He worked his mouth from side to side. "What about the name Bianca? And Victor Renard?"

She fisted her hands on the table in frustration. "Not really… Bianca doesn't feel right."

His mouth quirked up. "Well, we should know soon enough. We're running the DNA and your prints ASAP. Meanwhile, Officer Clemmens faxed me photographs of your husband's murder."

His look darkened as he opened the envelope and spread several photographs on the table.

Jane's pulse hammered at the sight of the man's bloody body. This man was supposed to be Victor, her husband.

She leaned closer and peered at his twisted arm and hand. The tattoo…it was there. The wolf…

Lone wolf… He'd given himself the nickname because he considered himself a loner.

But he'd definitely slipped the wedding ring on her finger. If he was a lone wolf, why had he decided to marry her?

The sheriff pointed to another photograph. This one of a .38. "This is the gun that killed Victor Renard," he said. "We're running the prints on the weapon and will compare to yours. The crime report from the scene revealed a hair strand was found, one that matches your color and length."

Of course they did, Jane thought. Everything, even the snippet of her memory, pointed to her as the killer.

He set a sheet of paper on the table. "This is a printout showing financial reports from Victor and Bianca Renard's account. It appears there are large sums of money that disappeared, payouts to an offshore account in the name of Sonja Simmons. Does that name sound familiar?"

"No," Jane said flatly.

"The policeman I spoke with believes she was Victor's lover, and that they were planning to disappear together." He produced another sheet with a photograph that resembled her. "He also discovered that you had another alias. Geneva Armstrong."

Jane didn't know what to make of the alias or any of this. "Let me guess," Jane said. "They think I killed Victor because he was leaving me for another woman."

Jacob lifted his shoulders in a small shrug. "It's a motive."

Jane kept her mouth shut. Somehow she didn't picture herself as a jealous woman. Or one who cared about money.

But it was difficult to argue with cold, hard evidence.

WATCHING HIS BROTHER interrogate Jane gnawed at Fletch's nerves. It had taken a half hour to convince Jacob to let him watch the interview, but he'd finally persuaded his brother he could read the nuances of Jane's expressions.

Jacob had stipulated that Fletch remain in the viewing room and not interfere.

It was getting more difficult every second to keep that promise.

Especially when Jacob was presenting such strong evidence against Jane. Evidence that made Fletch question whether he really knew her.

Jacob gestured toward one of the crime photos. "Do you recognize Victor Renard?"

Jane's face looked ashen. "Yes. And no."

"What does that mean?" Jacob asked bluntly.

Jane sighed and ran a hand through her hair. "I don't really remember him, but I had a nightmare about him. It was just a quick flash, but I saw his body bouncing backward as the bullet struck him."

Fletch swallowed hard. For the first time since Jacob had met them outside that cave, he realized Jane probably needed a lawyer.

"DID YOU SEE the murder weapon?" Jacob asked.

Jane cut her eyes toward the camera in the corner. Fletch shifted restlessly. Did she know he was watching?

Jacob leaned across the table, hands folded. "Did you see the gun, Jane?"

"I saw the gun dropping to the floor, but I don't remember seeing the shooter's face."

Jacob drummed his fingers on the table. "Victor was a real estate broker. He and Bianca worked together," Jacob paused. "Apparently they made millions in Florida and recently moved to North Carolina."

Jane sat unmoving, her shoulders squared.

Jacob removed another photo from the envelope and pushed it toward her. The photograph was an advertisement for Renard's Real Estate and Brokerage Company with a picture of her and Victor smiling side by side in front of a large Colonial house.

Her stomach fluttered as she examined it. "I... This can't be real."

Jacob crossed his arms. "What do you mean, it can't be real?"

Jane stared at him blankly, then a knock sounded on the door, and Jacob stood and went to answer it. Jacob's receptionist appeared at the door and spoke in a hushed tone.

He frowned, then turned, and walked back to the table. Anger hardened his voice as he began to shove the pictures back in the envelope. "I guess this interview is over. Apparently your lawyer has arrived."

Jane's brows shot up as if she hadn't expected the lawyer's appearance. "My lawyer?"

"That's what he said," Jacob replied. "I'll show him in."

Jane looked baffled as Jacob left the room, and Fletch hurried to talk to him.

He cornered him in the hallway before he

reached the front. "What's going on? Did Jane call a lawyer?"

"No," Jacob said. "But one showed up."

"Who is he?"

"I don't know. I'm going to meet him now."

As they stepped into the front reception area, a tall man with short dark hair stood by the receptionist's desk. He was slender and polished, his expensive suit and manicured nails screaming old money.

He buttoned the top button of his charcoal gray jacket, then extended his hand to Jacob. "Sheriff, my name is Woodruff Halls. I'm here about Bianca Renard."

As Jacob shook the man's hand, Fletch couldn't help but compare the two. Like Fletch's own hands, Jacob's were calloused and rough from doing hard work. This man's skin looked so smooth he'd probably never done a minute of physical labor in his life.

Jacob cleared his throat. "How did you know Jane Doe, the woman you call Bianca Renard, was here?"

Halls tapped his finger on his phone. "I spoke with Officer Clemmens." He adjusted his tie. "I also happen to know Mrs. Renard personally. She and her husband and I were friends. I understand Bianca is accused of murdering Victor, but I believe wholeheartedly in her innocence. That's the reason I rushed here. I don't intend to allow her to be tried and convicted for a crime she didn't commit. Or…to be assigned some legal aid attorney who has too many cases to investigate and represent her properly."

Fletch jammed his hands in the pockets of his jeans but kept his eyes trained on Halls. The man spoke with conviction, as if he strongly believed in Jane's innocence.

But Fletch still couldn't reconcile what he'd learned about Victor and Bianca to Jane. She didn't strike him as the type to care about money or fancy houses, or to hang around with men like Halls.

Of course he'd only known her for a few days, and in that time they'd been fighting to survive the blizzard and a hired gunman.

Jacob cleared his throat. "May I see your ID please?"

"Of course." Halls removed a business card from the top pocket of his jacket and handed it to Jacob. "Now I'd like to see my client, please."

Jacob gestured for Halls to follow him. He shot Fletch a look warning him to stay put. But Fletch didn't intend to stand by and let this guy take over without seeing Jane's reaction to him.

He waited until Jacob and the lawyer entered the interrogation room, then he hurried down the hall into the viewing room.

Jane's jaw worked as she swallowed, and when she raised her head to look at the lawyer, every muscle in her body stiffened. She went so still that for a moment, Fletch wondered if she was even breathing.

"Jane," Jacob said. "This man is Woodruff Halls. He claims he's representing you."

She folded her arms and offered the man a cool look.

Halls's tone turned curt. "I'd like to speak to my client in private." He gestured toward the small camera in the top corner of the room. "And shut that thing off."

Jacob held his arms by his sides, but Fletch recognized anger in the slight tensing of his body. "Jane?"

Her eyes turned to ice chips as she stared at Halls. Then she lifted her hand in a tiny motion signifying it was okay for Jacob to leave her alone with the man.

Fletch didn't like what was happening, but he felt helpless to stop it.

A second later, the TV screen blurred into snowy static, and he was left in the dark as to what was happening in that room.

JANE FELT AS if she was shutting down. She had no idea who this man who claimed to be her lawyer was.

But something about him sent chills up her spine.

"Bianca, or should I call you Jane?" the slickly dressed man asked.

"Jane for now," she said. *Bianca* still didn't feel right. Maybe she was in denial because she didn't want to believe that she was a cold-blooded killer.

"All right, Jane, I have to warn you that as of this moment, you talk to no one but me. Don't answer any more questions. Don't make any calls. Don't give in to the sheriff's pressure tactics and confess to something you may or may not have done."

Jane swallowed. "You think I killed this man Victor?"

Halls ran long, slender fingers through his gelled hair. "That's not what I said. But I'm advising you against a confession. Not until we exhaust all possibilities."

Anger simmered deep inside her, but she forced herself to be calm. "What do you know about Victor and his death?"

He pressed his lips into a thin line. "Just what the police have told me. But I understand you have amnesia, and we can use that to bargain for time. I've requested an emergency bail hearing for this afternoon so I can arrange for your release. Then we can explore your defense strategy."

He reached out and covered her hand with his.

A shudder coursed through Jane. Every bone in her body screamed that something was wrong here.

That this man wasn't who he claimed.

Chapter Fifteen

Fletch's stomach knotted as he watched Jane and her lawyer file into the courtroom. Due to Jane's amnesia, Halls had managed to finagle an emergency hearing with the local judge that afternoon.

He was relieved Jane wouldn't have to spend the night in jail, but the thought of her being released with nowhere to go disturbed him.

Jacob addressed the judge and read the charges. Halls stood and suggested bail be set and Jane be released into his custody.

"At this point, all evidence against my client is circumstantial and this woman is ill and does not appear to be a flight risk. I will personally assure the court that she will not flee the country and will be available for questioning when necessary. Meanwhile my client has agreed to enter a therapy program to help her regain her memory of the night in question."

The judge's hand shot up. "We are not here to try the case, Mr. Halls. But considering the extenuating circumstances, I agree the best course for obtaining justice is for Jane Doe to enter counseling. Bail is set at one hundred thousand dollars."

Halls smiled and adjusted his tie. "Thank you, Your Honor."

The judge pounded his gavel and dismissed the court. Jacob stood and Fletch moved up beside him. He silently willed Jane to look at him, but she didn't. She seemed stoic and resigned.

Halls escorted her to the court clerk to settle bail. "I don't like him," Fletch said in a low growl.

"Any specific reason?" Jacob asked.

Fletch scrunched his nose in thought. "I can't put my finger on it."

"Maybe you're just too close to the situation," Jacob said. "Too close to Jane."

Fletch made a low sound in his throat. "I guess since I found her, I feel protective of her," he admitted. "Part of my job. Now it's hard to walk away."

Jacob gave him a half-cocked smile. "You sure it was just the job?"

No, he wasn't. But he wasn't about to confess that he'd almost made love to Jane. That he still wanted to. That he'd fantasized about clearing her name and taking her to his house and spending all night giving her pleasure.

"Just check that lawyer out," Fletch said,

avoiding the question. "Make sure he's who he says he is."

"I plan to. And I'm still waiting on fingerprint and DNA results on Jane, as well as the evidence you brought in."

"Where do we stand on the bodies recovered from the trail?"

"Both men are at the morgue. Waiting on autopsies."

"Identifying them might tell us more about what happened," Fletch said.

While Halls posted bail, Fletch crossed the room into the hallway and called Jane's name.

She'd looked calm and composed in the courtroom, but he detected fear beneath that calm facade.

"Jane, do you recognize this lawyer?"

She shook her head. "He says he knows where I live, that he's driving me to my house." She gave a small shrug. "Going home might trigger my memories."

True. "I can go with you," Fletch offered.

Halls stepped over to join them. "That's not a good idea," Halls said. "Bianca, this man is the sheriff's brother. He could be fishing for information to share with the sheriff, information to use against you."

Jane's eyes flickered with unease as if she hadn't considered that possibility. Fletch gritted his teeth. Didn't she know him any better than that?

Halls took Jane's arm. "Come on, let's get you out of here. Being in your own environment might prompt a breakthrough with your memory loss."

Fletch rushed to catch up with them as Halls herded her out the door. Fletch slipped his business card into the pocket of her jacket. "He's wrong about me," he murmured close to her ear. "Call me if you need me."

Halls glared at him. "I thought I made myself clear, Mr. Maverick. Leave my client alone. She is to talk to no one but me."

Then he hustled Jane out the door toward a black Cadillac. A minute later, Halls drove away, carrying Jane with him.

JANE HAD DREADED spending the night in jail, but leaving with this virtual stranger intensified her feelings of trepidation.

When he'd addressed the judge, she had a sudden flashback. Halls was standing in the room with her when her husband had been shot.

But that didn't make sense. Was her mind playing tricks on her?

If Halls had been at the scene, did he know who'd killed her husband? If so, why hadn't he pointed the police in the direction of the real killer?

He steered his Cadillac out of town and veered onto the highway. "Where are we going?" Jane asked.

His cool gray eyes skated over her, then back to the road. "To your weekend house," he said. "Like I told the judge, being home might help trigger your memory of that night."

Jane twisted her hands together in her lap. "Is that where my husband was shot?"

He breathed out, low and steady. "Yes. You guys own a beautiful mountain cabin outside of Asheville."

"And I was an interior decorator?"

"That's right. You and Victor worked together."

Jane studied him. "What kind of law do you practice?"

He kept his eyes on the road as he sped around a curve. "Currently I handle divorce cases, but I litigated criminal cases early in my career."

But now he specialized in divorce? "How did you know me and Victor?" Jane asked. "Were we filing for a divorce?"

He tapped the steering wheel as he turned off the main highway onto the road leading toward Asheville. "No. Victor sold me my house, and you decorated it. You were such a power couple that I recommended your services to some of my acquaintances, then we became friends."

Jane worried her bottom lip with her teeth.

"You said you believe that I'm innocent. What about the evidence the sheriff had against me?"

"All circumstantial." He loosened his tie.

She latched on to that fact. "Tell me more about my relationship with Victor."

"You were madly in love with Victor, and he felt the same about you. Your marriage was stable. No infidelity on either part. In fact, you were planning a family."

They were? Jane mentally chastised herself. If they were so in love and planning a family, why couldn't she remember him or their wedding?

Because his death was too traumatic? Because she'd witnessed it?

"Nothing feels right," Jane said. "One of the few memories I have is the moment his body flew backward when the bullet pierced his chest."

Halls's breath punctuated the air. "So you witnessed the shooting?"

Jane shook her head. "I think so, but I don't remember the shooter's face, although…"

The car slowed as he maneuvered a turn, and he cut a sideways look at her. "Although what?"

Jane decided on the direct approach. "I thought you were there. I…saw you."

A vein throbbed in his neck. "You're obviously confused, Bianca. I have been to your house, but I was definitely not there the night Victor died."

His gray eyes skated over as if to say that was the end of the subject.

"Why don't you close your eyes and rest? It'll take about an hour to reach the house."

Jane's heart hammered. She didn't trust Halls. But hopefully when she revisited the place where Victor was killed, the past would come back to her.

"SOMETHING ABOUT THAT lawyer seems off to me," Fletch told Jacob.

Jacob chuckled. "Maybe you don't like the fact that Jane is with him and not you."

His brother had hit the nail on the head. Not that Jane was with him… "Can you run a background check on him?" Fletch asked. "Verify he's not some fake?"

"I'm on it as soon as we get back to the station," Jacob said. "I called Liam for help, too. He has resources that I don't."

Fletch thanked him, then they both climbed in their cars and drove back to the police station. He spoke to Jacob's deputy, Martin Rowan, and grabbed a cup of coffee on his way to Jacob's office. Jacob did the same, then sank in his desk chair and turned to his computer.

Jacob entered the name Woodruff Halls and ran a search. Fletch pulled a chair up to the desk and stared over Jacob's shoulder as information spilled onto the screen.

"He has no record, no arrests," Jacob said. "Here's his website. Halls Attorney at Law." The photograph of the lawyer was even more polished than the real man who'd appeared in court. Photoshop could do wonders these days.

Jacob maneuvered the site, and Fletch skimmed several reviews from clients, all glowing and praising his professionalism. Male clients seemed to be especially vocal about their settlements. Two had raved about how he'd stuck it to their cheating spouses.

Another section detailed criminal cases Halls had tried when he'd first graduated from law school. Nothing major, mostly petty crimes.

"He probably realized divorce cases were more profitable and switched specialties," Jacob muttered in disdain.

Fletch grimaced. On paper, the man was exactly who he claimed to be.

A knock sounded at the door and Liam poked his head in. "Hey, guys."

Jacob waved him inside, and Liam glanced at the computer screen.

"Just checked out the lawyer representing Jane Doe," Jacob said.

Liam gave them a grim look. "That's what I wanted to talk to you about."

Fletch's pulse jumped. His brother had answers. Hopefully to help clear Jane, not to prove her guilt. "Tell us what you learned."

Liam leaned one hip on the desk. "That's just

it. I didn't find anything on Bianca and Victor Renard."

"What do you mean?" Jacob asked. "No record of arrests on their part? Their business was legit, with no complaints?"

Liam rested his arm on his leg. "I mean I didn't find *anything*, as in no record that Bianca or Victor Renard even exist."

Fletch's response died in his throat.

"How is that possible?" Jacob pushed away from his computer. "The report I received about the missing person matching Jane Doe's description came from a police officer. So did copies of the prints and crime scene report."

Liam made a clicking sound with his teeth. "I don't know what's going on, Jacob. But I looked into that officer and he's been suspended for accepting bribes. He could have intercepted your inquiry about the missing persons, and responded with a fake report."

Fletch's mind raced.

A second later, panic seized him. "If Bianca and Victor Renard don't exist, why the hell did Halls show up to defend Jane? Why did he claim he knew them personally and that Jane was innocent?"

"Good question," Liam said.

Jacob coughed into his hand. "If Jane is not Bianca, who is she?"

Fletch stood, fear hacking away at his calm.

He'd started to believe that Jane had lied to him. That she was making a fool out of him as Hannah had done.

But this was different. Very, very different. Something was wrong.

Jane was in danger.

JANE STARTLED AS the car jerked to a stop. She was dazed and confused. She'd been dreaming about Fletch, not the shooting or her dead parents or other dead bodies and blood.

Halls veered onto a side road that led into deep woods. The hair on the back of her neck prickled.

"I thought we lived in a subdivision," Jane said, drawing on the fleeting pieces of memories she'd recovered.

Halls rolled his shoulders. "You own a house in a subdivision, but this was your second home, your private getaway."

Jane gripped the edge of the seat. Something about these woods seemed familiar. Yet strangely odd.

Ominous. Deserted.

"I'm not ready for this," she said, her voice cracking. "I…think I should go to a hotel for the night or at least to the house in the subdivision."

His voice grew icy. "I thought you wanted to remember what happened so you could clear your name."

Perspiration beaded on Jane's neck. "I do, but

the doctor warned me not to push it, that I would remember when I'm mentally ready."

The car bounced over ruts in the road, the woods swallowing them into the darkness as he drove down a narrow graveled road.

"Really, Mr. Halls—"

"It's Woodruff, Bianca." He covered her hand with his. His skin felt clammy, cold, and his reassuring squeeze made her skin crawl. "Remember, we're friends. And I'm here to help."

"Then please take me back," she said firmly. "I told you I'm not ready to do this."

He kept driving. "It may be difficult to face what happened, but once you remember who shot Victor, you'll thank me."

She doubted it. But it seemed futile to argue. He was barreling ahead, oblivious to her rising panic.

They drove deeper into the woods. A few cabins dotted the hills here and there. The towering trees and sharp ridges reminded her of when she'd been lost on the trail, running for her life.

Finally they reached a clearing where a small log cabin sat. The mountains rose in the background, tall and ominous-looking, as if the cabin had been built in the center of the ridges to offer privacy. Yet it was so secluded, it also seemed… dangerous.

Her skin prickled again. She didn't want to be isolated right now. She ached to be back with

Fletch, with people surrounding her, people she could trust.

"Here we are." The lawyer parked and slid from the vehicle, then walked around to the passenger side and opened the door.

Jane sat frozen in the seat, her chest aching with the effort to breathe.

"Come on, Jane, let's go inside."

Fear choked her. Halls reached for her hand, and she stared at the long, manicured fingers. That black signet ring with the gold *H* on it. Those fingers wrapped around a…gun…

Suddenly the world blurred…

A gunshot sounded, then a shout, and she saw her husband falling, blood spraying.

She screamed, turned and picked up the gun on the floor. But someone jumped her and threw her to the ground. The gun went off again, then she was clawing at the man on top of her, fighting him off.

"Bianca?"

A man's voice jarred her from the images, but when she looked up at the lawyer, she knew he had lied.

Halls had been there. His hands…that signet ring…

She had to get away from him.

She shoved her feet upward and kicked him, knocking him to the ground. Then she jumped over the console, started the engine again and peeled down the driveway.

Whoever Halls was, he wasn't her friend.

Chapter Sixteen

Jane pressed the accelerator and flew down the narrow road, gravel spewing from the lawyer's car.

Maybe she was making a mistake. Maybe she'd simply had an anxiety attack at the prospect of revisiting the scene of her husband's murder. Maybe Halls hadn't been at the scene of the shooting.

But the moment he'd walked into the interrogation room at the jail, an eerie sense that he was dangerous had overwhelmed her.

And that signet ring. She wasn't paranoid. He *was* there. He had lied.

She glanced over her shoulder to see if he was following. Thankfully she hadn't seen another car at the cabin, so he couldn't be behind her.

Relief rushed through her, and she maneuvered the turns through the woods until she connected to the main highway. She didn't know where she was going, only that she had to escape Halls.

She didn't trust him.

Without knowing who she was, she couldn't trust anyone.

Except... Fletch.

Halls's words about Fletch feeding information to his brother taunted her. He could be right.

Except she'd felt a connection between her and Fletch. A trust that she certainly hadn't felt with the lawyer.

She pressed the accelerator and checked over her shoulder again. He might have called the police on her. Traffic on the main highway buzzed by.

A siren wailed and she froze, body rigid as she glanced up and saw a police car zooming closer behind her.

Dear God, he had called the cops on her. Told them she was skipping bail. That she'd stolen his car.

She held her breath, slowed and pulled over into the right lane. A second later, the police car raced by.

Thank God.

Her hands felt clammy as she clenched the steering wheel. She had no idea where to go or what to do now.

Mentally, she tossed around different ideas as she drove toward Whistler. She could find a place and hide out. No. Running like a criminal would only make things worse. She wanted the truth, to know who she was.

And why someone wanted her dead.

Traffic thickened, and she fell into one lane, maintaining a steady speed so as not to attract attention.

She had to get rid of Halls's car. If he had reported it stolen, the police would be looking for it. Worse, they'd add auto theft to her murder charge.

Heart racing, she drove another thirty miles until she ventured into the farmland and countryside between Asheville and Whistler. Mountains rose, the snowcapped ridges gleaming in the light, a reminder that she'd almost died on the trail.

She would have if not for Fletch.

Making a snap decision, she scanned the exit signs for a place to get off. Then she could ditch this car and figure out what to do.

She steered Halls's Cadillac onto a dirt road not far from the next little town. Fear pulsed through her along with guilt.

She wasn't a criminal…she felt that in her bones. But she had to do what she had to do. Halls was dangerous. She just needed to prove it.

Desperate for answers, she rummaged through his car. Except for an overcoat and gloves, the back seat was empty. She searched his console and found some loose change and cash. Next she looked inside the dashboard.

Insurance, registration. A pack of cigarettes

and a lighter. Mints. A photograph. She pulled it out and looked at it. Halls's face stared back, but he wasn't alone. He was posed with a brunette about his age, his arm around her shoulders. The woman was attractive but looked stiff in the picture, as if she was unhappy about something.

Hmm. Must be his wife. She flipped the photograph and searched for a name. If she could talk to the wife, maybe she'd tell her if Halls was legit.

Or maybe she'd turn you in.

Hoping to find something helpful, she tugged her jacket around her and slid from the vehicle, then unlocked the trunk. She held her breath, half expecting to find a dead body inside. Maybe she'd watched too many horror movies.

No body, but she found a briefcase. She jimmied the lock and peered inside it. A couple of file folders containing papers and notes about divorce cases he was working on. Business cards.

She stuffed one of his cards in her pocket. Then she checked the side compartment and found another photo.

A picture of her and the man with the wolf tattoo on his arm. Her husband...

The world blurred, her legs buckling as emotions swirled inside her. Nausea rose to her throat, and she leaned against the car and bowed her head to stem the sick feeling. The ground seemed to open, and she felt as if she was falling into it, sliding deeper and deeper into a dark hole.

She pounded the car. Dammit, she wanted to see what was in that dark void.

Forcing air through her mouth, she fought through the nausea until the world finally righted again. Angry at her loss of control but more determined than ever to unearth her memories, she stuck the photograph in her jacket pocket, then shoved the briefcase back into the trunk and closed it.

Traffic noises from the highway echoed in the distance. She slipped past several boulders and walked along the shoulder of the narrow side road to the little town, ducking behind rocks and bushes as cars passed.

A sign for a coffee and pastry shop named The Bean caught her eye as she entered the town, and she walked up to the gas station beside it and asked if they had a pay phone.

An older man in overalls gestured toward an ancient-looking landline on the counter. "Long as it's not long distance, you're welcome to use it."

She thanked him then removed Halls's business card from her pocket and punched the number.

A minute later, a receptionist answered. "Andrea Horton, Halls Attorney at Law. How may I help you?"

"I'm trying to reach Mr. Halls's wife—"

"I'm sorry, but Mr. and Mrs. Halls are divorced. I couldn't divulge her personal contact information even if they were together."

Jane wondered exactly what had happened between them, but she didn't have a chance to ask. The line went dead in her hands.

FLETCH PACED JACOB'S OFFICE. "If Halls lied about Jane being Bianca Renard, what else did he lie about?"

Jacob pulled a hand down his chin. "Good question."

Liam phoned the lab and asked them to put a rush on Jane's fingerprints and DNA. "Do you have some results?" A pause, then Liam switched the caller to speakerphone.

"Yeah," Chad, the FBI analyst, said, "some info on the body of the man found on the rocks at Crow's Point."

"Go on."

"His name was Neil Akryn. PI out of a small town near Asheville."

Fletch, Jacob and Liam exchanged looks. "Did he work alone?" Liam asked.

"No, had a partner named Wiley Farmer. I put in a call to him but haven't heard back."

Liam's expression turned dark. "Have an officer check his office and home. See if they can locate him ASAP."

Fletch gritted his teeth as he waited.

"Ballistics from the bullet we removed from Akryn match the gun from your other dead man," Chad continued.

Liam made a clicking sound with his teeth. "So the man our Jane Doe shot killed Akryn?"

"Appears to be that way," Chad answered.

"Who is the man our Jane Doe shot?" Liam asked.

"Still working on his ID."

Liam snapped his fingers. "Officer Clemmens fabricated the evidence against Jane. But she recalls seeing a man she believes was her husband shot. Check morgues in and around Asheville and neighboring cities. See if any bodies turn up under the name of Victor Renard. And alert me as soon as the results of Jane Doe's prints and DNA are in."

"Will do."

Jacob furrowed his brows as Liam ended the call. "So what was a PI doing out on the trail? Looking for Jane Doe?"

Fletch shrugged. "Or Bianca? But we know Jane isn't Bianca." Fletch ran a hand through his hair. "And what's happening with Clemmens?"

"He disappeared, but our people are looking for him." Liam pinched the bridge of his nose. "Fletch, I need to know everything Jane told you while you were in those woods. Even the smallest detail might help solve this case."

Fletch sighed. "Let me grab some more coffee."

His brothers followed him for refills, and they carried their mugs back to Jacob's office.

Fletch sighed. "Before I found Jane, I saw blood in the snow. I followed it, then spotted a wedding ring in some bushes, then I found her. After I carried Jane to the shelter, it took her a while to regain consciousness. When she did, we finally talked. She recognized the ring, said she had a flashback of a man putting it on her finger, but she didn't remember a wedding or her husband's name." He touched the underside of his arm. "The husband had a tattoo of a wolf on his underarm near his wrist."

"Good detail. I'll have someone research that type of tattoo," Liam said. "What else?"

"When Jane was sleeping, she had nightmares about her parents' murder," Fletch said. "She was in her bedroom when she heard a noise. It sounded like someone breaking in. Then she heard gunshots. She hid in her closet for hours after the noise stopped and found her parents' bodies the next morning." He paused, disturbed by the image of a little girl discovering her parents' bloody corpses. "She was only twelve."

Jacob cursed. "That must have been traumatizing."

"A home invasion," Liam commented. "The question is was it random or was the couple targeted for a reason?"

Fletch cleared his throat. "She didn't remember, but she did say she thought her father was either a lawyer or a judge."

Liam worked his mouth from side to side. "Was the killer caught?"

Fletch shook his head. "That's all she told me about them."

"So we can't totally discount a connection to Jane's current situation?" Jacob muttered.

Liam folded his hands. "What would you estimate Jane's age to be now?"

"Early thirties. Maybe thirty-two, thirty-three?"

"That murder was bound to make the news. It's a long shot that it's related to Jane's current problems, but it will help narrow down her ID. I'll get someone on it right away."

"What else did she remember?" Jacob asked.

Fletch debated on how much to say. But they couldn't find the truth if he wasn't honest. His brothers were here to help. "She remembered seeing her husband's body flying backward and blood spewing, but she insists she didn't see the shooter's face."

A strained silence for a minute, then Liam shifted. "Tell us about the shooting with the bearded gunman. How exactly did Jane obtain your gun?"

Fletch hardened his jaw. "We were hiking and came upon the shelter at Stone's Ledge. I saw rope inside, and Jane recalled being tied and gagged and left there. She managed to untie herself and escape, but her attacker caught her. That's when he knocked her over the head and left her out in the storm to die."

"What a bastard," Jacob said.

Fletch gritted his teeth. "I collected the rope and bagged it, then we set off on the trail again. A little while later, we were ambushed. I grabbed Jane and we darted toward a boulder to take cover, but I took a bullet to the leg. As I fell, my gun slipped from my hand."

"Dammit, Fletch," Liam said. "You could have been killed."

"But I wasn't," Fletch said. "Then the man jumped Jane. She fought him off, grabbed my gun and shot him."

"She fought him off?" Jacob asked.

Fletch nodded. "I know it's hard to believe, but she had serious skills. Maybe from self-defense classes."

"And the shooting?" Liam asked. "She shot the man right between the eyes."

Fletch wiped sweat from the back of his neck. "It was impressive."

"She had experience, Fletch," Liam said. "Coupled with her fighting skills and marksmanship, it sounds like she had training in the military or…law enforcement."

Liam clenched his phone. "Let me text Chad and have him check military and police databases. If she had training either place, her prints will be in the system."

Fletch's phone buzzed on his hip, and he checked the number. Unknown. "I need to take this call. Work."

Fletch stepped from the room and quickly connected the call. "Hello."

"Fletch…" Jane's voice sounded breathless. "I'm in trouble. Please help me."

His blood turned to ice. "Where are you?"

She gave him an address somewhere between Whistler and Asheville. "Is Halls still with you?"

"No," Jane rasped. "He's not who he says he is. I…took his car and ran."

Relief momentarily filled him. "Good. Stay put. I'll be right there."

He didn't bother to tell his brothers where he was going, for fear they'd try to stop him. Instead he rushed past Jacob's receptionist and through the door. Outside, he jogged to his car, jumped in and peeled away.

He had to find Jane before Halls did.

JANE SAT HOLED up in the back of the tiny coffee shop, every nerve cell in her body on edge. She'd used the money in the console of Halls's car and bought one of the souvenir ball caps sporting the name of the town to wear as a disguise.

The waitress, a sweet young girl named Trish, approached, a pencil and order pad in her hand.

Trish's smile was big and wide, her lipstick a little too pink, with matching blush on her cheeks. Jane ordered plain coffee.

Trish insisted The Bean also served the best apple pie in the state. "Add a scoop of homemade vanilla ice cream on it and you'll think you died and went to heaven, honey."

Jane thanked her but politely declined. Her stomach was rolling too much to think about food.

Instead she noted the decor on the walls. Local artists' paintings depicted beautiful mountain scenes, fishing camps, hiking trails, white water rafting excursions, animals and the natural wonders of the forest.

A mixture of country and gospel music wafted through the room, and CDs by a local singer/songwriter was displayed by the cash register for sale. Trish and the owner, an older woman with wiry pink hair and a flour-dusted apron, greeted everyone who entered by name.

Except for her. She was the stranger. Alone. Trish had asked her what she was doing in Beaver Ridge, and she relayed the story she'd fabricated as a cover. She and her boyfriend were meeting for a romantic getaway at some cabins three miles north of Beaver Ridge. She'd noted the sign advertising the rental units on her way into town.

She'd left Halls's Cadillac parked a couple of

miles outside of the city limits on what appeared to be a deserted graveled road, and walked the rest of the way in.

Trish brought her a refill, and she was grateful she'd ordered decaf. Any more caffeine and her hands would be shaking like a leaf in the wind.

The wooden door opened, and two men in police uniforms loped in, both brawny and ominous-looking. Jane held her breath as one of them glanced around the café, then they scooted onto the barstools at the coffee counter.

Jane tugged the ball cap lower on her head and angled herself so she could watch them without looking conspicuous. They ordered coffee and, no surprise, the pie with ice cream, then chatted with Trish while they waited on their orders.

Jane felt like a criminal on the run. She didn't like it, but she had to lay low until she could prove her innocence.

While she sipped her coffee, she jotted down the details she knew so far about herself on a napkin. Bianca and Victor Renard's name went next, then Woodruff Halls. She wished she had a computer so she could do some digging on her own.

A loud static sound cut through the silence, and she realized the officer was receiving a call. The taller one snagged his piece and responded.

Jane strained to overhear the conversation.

"Stolen vehicle belonging to Attorney Woodruff Halls, 2019 Black Cadillac, License LW2FU, found on Old Salter Road outside of Beaver Ridge. Party responsible thought to be wanted…"

The words faded and the officer glanced across the room again. Fear seizing her, Jane left a ten on the table, then slid from the booth, hunched low and darted toward the rear exit.

Voices echoed behind her, but she didn't look back. She dashed around the corner of the building into the alley and started to run.

Chapter Seventeen

Fletch's pulse pounded as he rolled into Beaver Ridge. He immediately spotted The Bean, where Jane was supposed to be waiting on him, and exhaled in relief.

Although relief vanished when he noticed the police car parked in front. Damn, had Halls reported that Jane had jumped bail? If the man was involved in the crime Jane was accused of committing, why would he tip off the police?

Halls had also met Jacob at his station and appeared in front of a judge.

Pretty audacious to put his face in front of law enforcement if he was trying to hurt Jane.

Praying the cops hadn't found Jane and arrested her, he cruised into the parking lot and swerved into a spot. He quickly surveyed the area. Several cars were in the lot, patrons coming and going.

No Jane.

Willing himself to remain calm, he remembered the cover story Jane had invented and climbed from his vehicle. He kept his senses honed as he crossed the parking lot to the entrance.

By the time he reached it, two cops loped outside, one on his radio, the other jangling his keys.

"We'll canvass the area," the officer informed Dispatch.

They both jumped in the squad car, and the driver started the engine and backed from their parking spot. Fletch pretended he was deep in conversation on his phone as he passed them.

Before he went inside the café, though, he once again surveyed the parking lot. No Halls. No Jane, either.

The scent of cinnamon, apple pie and strong coffee engulfed him as he entered. The coffee shop was full of mountain charm, a testament to the local artists and an invitation to visitors to explore the area.

People gathered in booths with red checked tablecloths; a seating area near the front boasted a couch and several lounging chairs, and the bar provided seating for individuals and takeout orders.

He scanned the room for Jane but didn't see her at a table or booth. A young waitress sauntered over and smiled up at him. "Hi, I'm Trish. You can sit anywhere, sir. I'll take your order when you're ready."

"Actually I was supposed to meet a young

woman here," Fletch said, returning the girl's friendly manner.

Trish's eyes brightened. "Your girlfriend?"

Either she was fishing or she'd spoken with Jane. "That's right. A pretty brunette. We're planning a romantic getaway in the mountains—"

"In those cabins," the girl finished with a grin. "She told me about it. How nice."

Fletch shifted and looked across the room again. "I guess I might be too early?"

"No. She was right back here." Trish walked toward the rear of the shop and paused at the last booth where a half-full coffee mug still sat. "Well, darn, this was her booth."

Fletch pressed his hand over his phone, willing Jane to call. "Would you mind checking the ladies' room for me?"

"Of course not." Trish turned at the end of the hall and ducked inside the ladies'. A second later, she came out, her brows furrowed. "No, not in there. Maybe she stepped out for some fresh air or to grab some souvenirs."

"Probably. I'll give her a call." He squeezed her arm. "Thanks, Trish."

Fletch noticed the back exit. If Jane saw the police officers inside, she might have gotten nervous and left out the back.

He waited until Trish moved to the next booth to take an order, then he hurried through the exit and began to search the alley.

JANE DARTED DOWN several alleys, staying in the shadows, keeping low and out of sight as traffic crawled through the sleepy little town. But even as she ran from the police, she knew she couldn't run forever.

She might not remember her name, but she wasn't a coward. She had to face this situation head-on.

Still, she wasn't ready to go back to jail. Although Fletch might turn her in to his brother, it was a chance she was willing to take.

The police car that had been parked at the café suddenly zoomed by. She released a breath, trying to ignore the acrid odor of garbage, rotting food and stale beer permeating the alleyway.

Knowing Fletch was supposed to meet her at the coffee shop, she turned back toward The Bean.

The rear door of one of the shops opened, and two employees stepped outside and lit up cigarettes. The scent of smoke mingled with the foul garbage odors, and she hurried away. She wove between two other stores until she had a vantage point to the coffee shop parking lot.

Fletch's Wrangler was parked toward the back of the lot beneath a live oak. Jane's breath quickened, and she scanned the area for signs someone was watching. More police could be looking out.

Or Halls. He'd had enough connections to get

her bail hearing moved up. What if he had other connections with the law?

She wished like hell she had his cell phone. But he'd had it clipped to his belt and in her haste to escape, she hadn't thought about grabbing it.

She rubbed her temple to regroup.

Seconds ticked by. The feeling that she needed to escape Halls didn't dissipate. The feeling that she wanted to see Fletch didn't, either.

She opened her eyes and glanced across the parking lot again. Two young women and their babies strolled into The Bean. No cops. No one lingering in the parking lot, looking suspicious.

Deciding it was now or never, she ducked low, slinking between a place called the Burger and Brew and Carlos's Cantina. She gripped the edge of the concrete wall and watched. Waited. The coast was clear.

Just as she lunged forward to break into Fletch's Jeep Wrangler, to hide and wait for him, someone grabbed her from behind.

She started to fight, but a hand covered her mouth and a firm muscled arm gripped her around the waist, pressing her so tightly against the man's body that she could barely breathe.

God help her. Had Halls found her?

"BE STILL, IT'S all right," Fletch said in a low whisper. "It's me."

Jane froze, her body trembling.

"I'm going to release you," he said into her ear. "Trust me, okay?"

She gave a little nod, and he moved his hand from her mouth and loosened his hold. Her body sagged in relief against him, and she turned in his arms and shoved at him.

Her eyes were wide, dark with anger. "You scared me to death."

"I'm sorry," he said and meant it. "I didn't mean to."

Her chest rose and fell on a labored breath, and she planted her hands on her hips. "There were cops here. Did you call them?"

Fletch felt as if he'd been slapped. "No, Jane. I told you that you could trust me."

"They're looking for me, for Halls's Cadillac," she said, her breathing unsteady.

Fletch scanned the alley, then the parking lot. "Come on, let's get in my Jeep. Then we can talk."

Jane's lower lip quivered. "You're not carrying me back to Jacob, to jail?"

"No," Fletch said earnestly. "But we do need to talk."

Jane's gaze shot to his Jeep as if gauging the distance. Anxious, she started to run, but Fletch caught her and curved his arm around her shoulders. "Hold on. Remember we're a couple on a romantic getaway. We don't want to draw attention."

Jane's eyes brightened. "You're right." She slid her arm around his waist and leaned into him. "Thank you for coming."

Fletch offered her a smile, but his heart was pounding. He wanted the romance to be real. For them to be a couple. For her to be safe and this mess tied up so they could figure out if there was really something between them.

Together they sauntered toward his Jeep, hugging and taking their time so as not to arouse suspicion. When they reached the Jeep, Fletch unlocked the door and Jane slid inside. Just for show, or at least that was what he told himself, he leaned over and gave her a kiss.

Jane's breath caught when he pulled away, a seed of longing sprouting. Or maybe it was surprise. Either way, he closed the door and smiled to himself as he walked around to the driver's side.

A few seconds later, they were buckled up, and he guided his Jeep back onto the highway.

Jane twisted her hands together and stared out the window as if she might find answers somewhere in the ridges and forests. "Where are we going?" she finally asked.

Fletch gritted his teeth. He should call Jacob and Liam. And he would. Just not yet.

"My place," Fletch said. "No one will look for you there."

Except his brothers. And he'd handle them if he had to.

JANE PRESSED HER fingers to her lips. Fletch's kiss taunted her with what-ifs. What if she wasn't mired in a murder investigation? What if someone wasn't trying to kill her?

What if she and Fletch could run away together, for forever?

He hit a pothole, and she winced. *Get a grip. Running isn't the answer.*

But it sure as hell was tempting right now.

Fletch remained silent as he drove, his jaw firmly set. She closed her eyes and forced herself to analyze the shooting and Halls's behavior.

None of it made sense, especially the fact that she kept dreaming of her parents' murder as if it had something to do with the mystery riddling the present.

Her parents had been killed around twenty years ago. She was almost certain the killer had been caught and locked away.

The strain of the day took its toll, and she must have fallen asleep because sometime later, she woke with a start. Fletch's Wrangler bounced over ruts in the road, spewing gravel as he drove down a narrow road into the woods.

For a moment, fear prickled at her. The place looked isolated, far away from the town.

She swallowed hard. God help her, she *was* paranoid. Fletch had saved her life and been nothing but good to her. They'd depended on each other in the wilderness. She had to trust him now.

He parked in front of an A-frame log cabin with a picture window that occupied the entire front of the house. A chimney and the rustic features gave it an inviting feel. Trees, bare of leaves, snaked across the back, climbing into the snow-capped mountains.

"It's beautiful," she murmured.

"I like it," Fletch said, a hint of pride in his tone. "Let's go inside and talk."

Jane opened her car door and climbed out. Mounds of snow and melting slush covered the ground. The sound of river water rippling over rocks echoed from behind Fletch's cabin. He led the way up to his front porch, unlocked the door and stepped inside, flipping on lights as he entered.

Jane followed, awed by the stacked-stone fireplace running from floor to ceiling. A black leather sectional and a blue-and-green braided rug made the room look masculine, but homey and warm. Paintings of the wilderness adorned the wall, and an acoustic guitar leaned against the big club chair by the fireplace.

She imagined Fletch strumming a country song with the firelight flickering off his chiseled jaw, and her body hummed with need.

He walked straight to a wet bar situated in the built-ins flanking the fireplace. "Wine or scotch?" he offered.

"Scotch," Jane said. She wasn't sure she liked it, but the answer came so quickly that she must.

He poured them both two fingers into a tumbler, lit the gas logs, then gestured for her to sit on the sofa. She did and he joined her, then handed her the drink. Jane's hand trembled.

He took a swallow of his scotch, then pinned her with his dark chocolate eyes. "What happened with Halls?" he asked in a tone tinged with barely suppressed anger.

"He lied to me, to you," she said. "He's not who he says he is. And I don't think we were friends."

Fletch heaved a wary breath. "Go on."

"Like I said before, I saw an image of the man with the tattoo, my husband, being shot, his body bouncing backward." She licked her dry lips. "Then the gun. It was in my hand, but I don't remember shooting it."

She hadn't mentioned that detail before.

"Halls was there," Jane said. "In the room when Victor was shot."

Fletch's fingers curled around the arm of the sofa. "You're sure?"

Jane nodded. "Yes, I'm certain of it."

"Did he admit this?" Fletch asked.

Jane ran her finger around the rim of her glass. "No, that's just it. He completely denied it, claimed he'd been in the house visiting before, but that he wasn't there when Victor died. He insisted I was confused." Her nerves pinged just thinking about being in the car with him. "I know I've been confused, but I'm not confused about this, Fletch. I saw his face. And every instinct in my body screamed that he's dangerous."

"What else happened?"

"He drove me to a remote cabin that he claimed belonged to me and Victor. I...don't think that was true, either. When we passed this cluster of rocks shaped like a cactus, I got chills. None of it feels right, Fletch."

She rubbed her arms with her hands. "When he parked and got out, I had a flash of him shooting Victor. I panicked. Then I shoved him, took his car and drove away as fast as I could. When I reached that town, I called you."

Fletch's silence unnerved her even more. Did he believe her?

"He probably reported his car stolen," she said. "That's why the police were looking for me at the coffee shop."

Fletch tossed back the rest of his drink, then set his tumbler on the coffee table and gripped her arms. "You were right not to trust him,"

Fletch said. "His story about Bianca and Victor Renard doesn't pan out."

Jane's breath quickened. "What do you mean?"

"My brother Liam, with the FBI, investigated the Renards. Jane, there is no Bianca or Victor Renard."

Jane's head swirled with confusion. "Then I'm—"

"I don't know who you are, but your name is not Bianca," Fletch said.

Jane's pulse clamored. "I didn't think that name felt right."

"If Halls lied about your identity, he may have lied about everything else."

"But I do remember a ring and a man being shot," Jane said. "And Halls was there."

"Then it's possible Halls *is* the one who shot the man. You witnessed it, and he's framing you."

"If that's true, who was the bearded man I shot? And why was he trying to kill me?"

"Still waiting on information on him," Fletch said. "But the dead man with the scarred face was a PI. He may have been hired by Halls."

"What motive would Halls have to kill my husband?"

"That's what we're going to find out. Liam is putting a rush on your prints and DNA. Soon, we should know who you really are."

"I still don't understand, though. Your brother had all that evidence against me."

"Liam discovered Officer Clemmens faked that information. He could be in cahoots with Halls somehow and fabricated it to make you look guilty."

A sick feeling slithered through Jane. "Then Halls came to my rescue and bailed me out so he could silence me."

"Elaborate but feasible." Disgust laced his tone. "I guess he thought Whistler had some country bumpkin cop who wouldn't check things out. His mistake."

Jane threw back the rest of her drink. Questions lingered, the future uncertain. She held all those answers inside her head, obliterated as if they'd been erased like words on a whiteboard.

"Jane?"

She offered him a tentative smile. "Thank you for helping me, Fletch. I…didn't know where else to turn."

His dark gaze raked over her, sending a tingle of awareness through her. Then he angled his head and tilted her chin up with his thumb. "I'm glad you trusted me."

Tears threatened, but she blinked them away. He moved closer, his mouth only inches from hers. Jane wanted him so badly she ached.

"Fletch, we shouldn't…not until we know who I am."

He grunted, a small sound of frustration underscored with need and desire. "I don't care what your name is. I know who you are, and you're not a murderer."

An image of her hand holding that gun haunted her. But then Fletch's lips touched hers, and she blocked out the image as hunger overcame her, and she pressed her lips to his.

Chapter Eighteen

Fletch lost all rational sense when Jane's lips melded with his. When they learned her identity, there might be a dozen reasons she wouldn't, or couldn't, be with him.

Another man. A child.

But he banished those possibilities for the moment.

When he'd watched Halls drive away with her, it had done something to him. Scared him because he didn't know the man or what would happen with Jane.

Scared him because he wanted her with him.

He'd never felt this way about a woman before.

He didn't like this desperate need, but he couldn't deny his feelings for her, either. Was this how Jacob had felt when he'd fallen for Cora? She'd seemed unstable to some folks, but Jacob had recognized she was suffering, and love made them both feel whole again.

Cora kept a magnet on their fridge that boasted the phrase *Live in the Moment*.

That was exactly what he wanted to do now.

Jane murmured a low sound of desire, and he deepened the kiss, tasting her sweetness and passion as he thrust his tongue inside her mouth. She raked her hands through his hair and drew him closer, and he pulled her up against him. Her soft breasts pressed against his chest, heightening his hunger.

He tore his mouth from hers and trailed wicked tongue lashes along her throat and around her ear. She moaned and clawed at the buttons on his shirt until she opened one, then the other. Her hands dove between the folds of the fabric, then she raked her nails over his bare skin.

Enflamed with passion, he nibbled at her neck, then tugged at her sweater. She lifted it over her head and tossed it onto the chair, then reached for him. But he held her arms by her sides so he could look at her.

She was beautiful. The bruises were fading on her creamy skin and her breasts swelled over the lacy bra. He wanted her breasts in his hands.

He wanted everything off so nothing separated them. Bare skin to bare skin.

Heat flared in her eyes, and she lowered her head and flicked her tongue against his nipple. He'd never realized how sensitive they were until she ran her tongue over each one then tugged one between her teeth and sucked it just as he wanted to do her.

"Hell, woman," he moaned.

She trailed her fingers lower to the waistband of his jeans and unsnapped them. He moaned and captured her hand in his. If he didn't slow down, he was going to explode before he was inside her.

He stood, his voice commanding, raw hunger pulsing through him. "Come on." Afraid his leg would give way if he tried to carry her, he tugged her hand and coaxed her to his room.

He paused in the doorway and lifted her chin to study her, to make sure this wasn't one-sided.

"I want you, Jane."

"I want you, too, Fletch." Desire flickered in her eyes, the same kind of desperate hunger mounting inside him. His body was wound tight with sexual tension. His sex throbbed.

He kissed her again, deep and hard, then walked her back toward the bed. She pulled off his shirt and reached for his jeans.

He shucked them, and in seconds had her naked in his bed, just as he wanted.

EVERY NERVE CELL in Jane's body was on sensory overload. Hunger and need built inside her as Fletch trailed his fingers over her breasts and belly.

His lips came next, painting a sensual trail over her bare body. Her nipples stiffened to peaks, and he teased them with his tongue then drew one into his mouth, firing liquid heat all the way to her womb.

She raked her nails over his back, feeling his corded muscles tighten as he crawled above her. He sucked one turgid peak, then the other, a throbbing ache consuming her.

She wanted him. Naked. Hard. Inside her.

He'd already done away with her panties, and she parted her legs, begging for his body to join with hers. Instead, he trailed his tongue down her belly to her heat. Then he nudged her legs further apart and pressed his lips to her slick, wet center.

She moaned and gripped his shoulders as he dipped his tongue inside her and teased her unmercifully. A flick of his tongue to her sweet spot, then another and another, and she lifted her hips and urged him to come inside her.

But he had his own agenda, and he tormented her with his mouth and fingers until pleasure shivered through her.

Finally Fletch climbed above her, reached into his nightstand, removed a condom and ripped open the package. Seconds later, she helped him roll it on.

He kissed her again and stroked her hot spot with his thick length. She parted her legs, aching for him to make love to her. He entered her in one quick thrust, filling her completely, then pulling out and thrusting into her body again.

Time after time, he teased her opening with

his shaft, then plunged his erection inside her until they built a frenetic rhythm. Slick, hot skin against slick, hot skin.

Teasing. Filling. Big. Hard. Her body quivered with sensations that mounted and made her ache for more.

She clawed at his firm backside, driving him deeper, then wrapped her legs around his waist. He suckled at her neck, and another orgasm teetered on the surface.

Fast. Hard. Deep. Over and over again until she spun into a world of pleasure. His big body went tense, still for a moment, then a guttural groan sounded as if it was ripped from his gut.

A minute later, his body shook as his own pleasure overcame him.

Jane clenched his hips as he pushed deeper into her and colors exploded behind her eyes.

Fletch's ragged breathing mingled with hers in the aftermath of their lovemaking, their bodies slick with perspiration and heat.

She stroked his back, savoring his strong body on top of her.

"Ahh, Jane," he said on a rough whisper. "I don't know who you are or what you do to me, but I can't stop myself from wanting you."

A smile formed on her lips, and she kissed him hungrily. She didn't know what had come over either of them, but she wanted their lovemaking to go on forever.

Although reality threatened to intercede and brought guilt. Had she felt this strongly about the man who'd put that wedding ring on her finger?

Should she be planning his funeral and honoring him instead of crawling into bed with another man?

FLETCH SENSED JANE'S tension but cradled her in his arms and soothed her by whispering nonsensical words. His body still zinged with passion in the aftermath of their lovemaking.

He didn't want to release her. Not yet. Maybe never.

"Are you going to tell your brothers I'm here?" Jane whispered.

Fletch angled his head to study her. "Do you want me to?"

Jane traced her finger over his bare chest. "I suppose it's not fair to ask you to hide me."

Fletch chuckled. "None of this is fair." He touched her bruised wrists. "It wasn't fair that someone tied you up and tried to kill you."

Jane nodded against him. "Tonight, can we just stay here alone?"

Fletch wanted time as much as she did. "Yeah. Jacob and Liam are working on your case. Liam put a rush on your prints and DNA at the lab so hopefully tomorrow you'll know some answers."

Relief and anxiety reverberated in Jane's slow

exhale. "Then we figure out everything else," she said softly.

"That's right." He only hoped the truth didn't send her back to jail.

She nestled against him, and he wrapped his arms around her, and she fell asleep in his arms, safe for the night.

The idea of seeing Jane locked away for the rest of her life made his stomach coil. He'd definitely crossed the line and let his emotions get the better of him with Jane.

But he had to believe that things would work out.

Nothing that felt this good could be wrong, could it?

Finally exhaustion sucked him into a restless slumber. He startled awake a few hours later with early morning sunlight streaming through the window. Jane looked so peaceful and sexy in his bed that he dropped a kiss on her forehead and memorized her features, afraid today might take her away from him.

Another possible theory occurred to him as he slipped from bed and brewed a pot of coffee. What if there wasn't any information on Victor and Bianca Renard because they were in WIT-SEC? That might explain the reason Jane had an assumed name. It might also explain the images she'd mentioned of those dead people.

She might have witnessed a crime, entered

witness protection, then killed this man Victor because he turned on her. The same with the two guys in the woods.

But how did the lawyer play into it? Had he killed her husband, or had he represented her to the Federal Marshals and helped arrange her new identity?

JANE WOKE TO the heavenly scent of coffee brewing. At first, she was disoriented, but she rolled over and saw sunlight streaming through the window. The bed beside her was empty.

Fletch.

She was in his house, in his bed. They'd made love last night. And it had been wonderful.

But what would happen today?

She rose and slipped on one of his shirts lying on the chair, buttoned it up, then tiptoed to the bathroom and washed her face. She ran her fingers through her tangled hair, loosening the knots as she examined her image in the mirror.

The bruises were fading, but she still had some discoloration on her forehead. Her eyes looked brighter and more rested, although her forehead wrinkled into a frown. For all she knew about herself, she might as well be looking at a stranger's face in the mirror.

"Who are you, Jane?" she whispered. "And who was this woman Bianca?"

The sound of Fletch's footsteps brought her

from the bathroom, and she walked through the bedroom and yanked on socks, then stepped into the living room. The strong scent of coffee wafted toward her, luring her into the kitchen.

Fletch stood on his back deck, facing the beautiful mountains, a mug in his hand. An extra one sat on the counter, so she filled it and carried her cup out to the deck.

Her breath caught at the sight of the snowy ridges, then the rippling river water below. The sight of Fletch's handsome chiseled body sent a hot flame of desire through her.

"Morning." Fletch tilted his head to look at her, his sexy eyes meeting hers as if searching for regrets.

She had none, at least not about sleeping with him. "Morning." She warmed her hands by cradling the hot coffee. "Thanks. I may not remember my name, but I think I'm a coffee addict."

A sly grin tugged at his mouth. "Me, too."

For a moment they stood still, sipping their coffee and simply enjoying the scenery.

"This place is breathtaking," she murmured.

"Thanks. I had it built," Fletch said. "Once Mom and Dad died, the four of us decided to build our own places. Too many memories at the old homestead."

"And I have hardly any," she said.

"Sorry, that was insensitive."

"No, you were being honest. And I have to

recover my past in order to clear my name and have a future," she said earnestly.

"You will." Fletch leaned against the deck rail, almost pensive. "I was thinking about possible theories this morning, trying to fit the random clues together. The fake name Bianca, your memory of seeing dead bodies, the men trying to kill you. We talked before about you possibly witnessing a crime. What if that is the case, and you entered WITSEC until you could testify?"

Jane massaged her temple. WITSEC would explain her name change, and could mean she wasn't a killer.

"I texted Liam and asked him to consult with the Federal Marshals."

A knock sounded on Fletch's front door. Jane jerked her gaze to Fletch. "Did you tell anyone I was here?"

He shook his head. "No. Go into the bedroom and stay while I see who it is."

Nerves pinged inside Jane as she hurried into Fletch's bedroom. She closed the door and locked it, then pressed her ear to the flat surface to listen to the conversation. Through the slit in the door-jamb, she watched two of his brothers storm in.

"What in the hell is going on, Fletch?" Jacob barked.

Fletch ran his hands through his hair. "What do you mean?"

Jacob strode through the room, looking around

as if he was searching for something. "That damn lawyer called me. He said Jane assaulted him and stole his car."

Fletch crossed his arms. "If she did, she must have had a good reason." He turned toward Liam. "What about the WITSEC angle?" Fletch said, dodging his brother's question.

A chill went through Jane, and she snatched her clothes and quickly dressed.

"I've got calls into the Federal Marshals and am waiting to hear back," Liam said. "But they don't share information easily, even to the FBI."

"Listen to me, little brother," Jacob continued. "At this point, Jane is considered a fugitive. She jumped bail, assaulted a man and stole his car. If you're hiding her, then you can be charged with aiding and abetting a felon," Jacob bellowed. "Perhaps even as an accomplice to murder."

Oh, God. Jane couldn't let Fletch get in trouble because of her.

She couldn't find the truth if she was locked in a cell, either. And it sounded as if Jacob had already convicted her in his mind.

Panic and reason warred inside her. She had to return to that cabin and see if being there triggered her memories. But going back would be dangerous.

She rushed to Fletch's pack and removed his weapon. She grabbed an extra magazine and put it in her pocket with the gun.

Tiptoeing, she ducked out the sliders leading to the back deck, then jogged down the steps into the woods.

She'd find a ride somehow, then she'd face her demons. The memory of Fletch making love to her taunted her.

She had to protect him. And that meant going alone.

Chapter Nineteen

Fletch inhaled a deep breath. "I thought you suspected Halls was lying."

Jacob and Liam exchanged looks. "Your theory about WITSEC made me start thinking," Liam said. "Halls could have worked with Jane to enter her into the program."

Fletch jammed his hands in his pockets. "I considered that possibility, but if so, why didn't he tell us that?"

Liam cleared his throat. "Part of the reason WITSEC works is the safety and security it provides for the witness. That means extremely limited access to information regarding the person, their new identity and their location. All communication between family, friends or former coworkers is completely cut off."

"I understand that," Fletch said. "But Jacob is law enforcement."

"One leak, even unintentional, can endanger the person in the program," Liam said.

Fletch scratched his head. "We need to talk to

Halls. Force him to tell us what's going on. If he arranged for Jane to enter WITSEC, then he has information about the crime she witnessed and who's after her."

"I'll contact him and ask him to meet us," Jacob offered.

Liam leaned against the kitchen island. "Did Jane tell you anything else, Fletch?"

Fletch considered confiding that Jane thought Halls had been at the murder scene, but he wasn't ready to reveal she was hiding in his bedroom.

She trusted him and he wanted to keep it that way.

So he opted for focusing on the couples she'd seen in her nightmares. "She also had dreams where she saw the faces of men and women who'd been murdered. Married couples."

Liam went very still. "Couples?"

Fletch nodded. "A man and woman lying together, dead. She said it was just flashes of images, that it could have been photographs from the news."

Liam drummed his fingers on the bar. "The FBI is investigating a case involving married couples being murdered. What if Jane witnessed one of them?"

Fletch crossed his arms. "That sounds feasible."

Jacob shifted. "But how does her husband play into it?"

"Maybe he was the killer," Fletch said. "She could have found out what he did or saw him kill one of the couples and confronted him. He came after her to silence her, then she killed him in self-defense."

"All possibilities," Liam admitted. "Although just theories at this point." He snapped his fingers. "Let me see what I can find out." He removed his phone from his belt and stepped onto the deck to make a phone call.

Jacob tapped his phone. "I'll call Halls and see if I can convince him to come in."

Fletch nodded as Jacob made the call. He placed it on speaker, but Halls's voice mail picked up, so Jacob left a message saying it was urgent he return his call.

Fletch watched Liam pace the deck as he talked. He paused by the table and stared at the coffee mugs on the table.

Two of them.

Dammit.

A second later, Liam strode in, jaw set, eyes flaring with suspicion. "She's here, isn't she, Fletch? You've been hiding her and lying to us ever since we arrived."

GUILT NAGGED AT Jane as she darted through the woods. She hated leaving Fletch in the lurch, but she cared too much about him to cause him trouble with his family. He'd suffered enough anguish with his parents' deaths.

Her memory loss, the past, the shooting—they were her problems.

She dealt with her problems on her own. She had to. She had no one to rely on.

She halted for a moment, the realization that she was truly alone clear in her mind. She had never been married.

So who was the man who'd put the ring on her finger?

Shaken, but hoping for another breakthrough, she followed the river east toward the outskirts of Whistler to the road leading out of town. Logic warred with panic. She needed transportation.

A car whizzed by and her stomach somersaulted. Not knowing who was after her made her hesitant to climb in a vehicle with a stranger.

Another car rumbled behind her, and she dove behind some bushes to hide until it passed. As soon as it sped by her, she began walking again, ears peeled for other cars approaching as she followed the road.

Two-foot snowdrifts still stood along the side of the road. Melted snow and ice clogged the shoulder, forcing her to tread more slowly than she wanted. Finally she spotted a farm complete with a barn and a couple of horses and cows in the pasture.

The house was set back down a mile-long

drive, but an old truck sat abandoned near the road with a For Sale sign tacked on the windshield.

She scanned the drive and road but didn't see anyone watching so she opened the driver's door and slid in. The seats were worn, the truck battered. She just prayed it would start.

No keys in the ignition. Instinctively, she checked the vehicle but found nothing, so she hotwired the engine. It purred softly, bringing a relieved smile to her face. On the heels of relief came the question—how had she known how to hotwire a car?

She didn't have time to dwell on that question, though. The owner could appear any minute.

She shifted into Drive, pressed the accelerator and veered onto the road. An old farm hat lay on the seat, so she picked it up and jammed it on her head as a disguise.

Knowing Fletch and his brothers might be looking for her, and the truck owner might report his truck stolen, she maintained a steady speed limit so as not to draw attention.

The country road was practically deserted, with only an occasional car and a couple of eighteen-wheelers passing by. A few more miles, and a truck carrying crates of live chickens zoomed past, heading in the opposite direction.

She wasn't sure she remembered how to find the cabin where Halls took her, but as she drove,

she searched for landmarks she'd noticed on the
drive. A horse farm. Sign advertising strawberry
picking, although that was out of season. Signs
for apple orchards a little farther north.

A siren suddenly blared, and she glanced in
her rearview mirror, dread curling in her belly.
She searched for a side road to turn onto, but
there was nothing.

The wailing grew louder. She maintained her
speed, praying the police weren't after her.

Blue lights twirled in the sky, the siren taunting her as the police car grew closer and closer.

"What the hell?" Liam snapped. "We're helping you and you're lying to us."

"Look, I was going to tell you," Fletch said.
"But I wanted to know if you had information
first."

Jacob glared at him. "Where is she?"

Fletch hurried to block the way as Jacob barreled toward the bedroom.

"Don't tell me you slept with her," Liam said
darkly.

Fletch held up a hand to prevent them from
storming in. "Let me explain. She came here last
night. She was scared, said when Halls drove her
to the house she and her husband supposedly
lived in, she knew something was wrong. That
he was lying. She was afraid of him, and didn't

want to go inside with him, so she took his car and drove to a coffee shop to meet me."

His brothers frowned in disapproval.

"Why was she afraid of him? Did he say something? Try to hurt her?" Liam asked.

Fletch gritted his teeth. "She remembered seeing him at the house when her husband was shot. She thought he killed her husband and framed her."

Jacob heaved a breath. "Or maybe he showed up to consult with her after the shooting and tried to help her enter WITSEC like we discussed."

"Tell her to come out here," Liam ordered. "We have to talk."

Fletch wanted to protect Jane. But the only way to do that was to uncover the truth. So he knocked on the bedroom door, then eased it open.

The sight of the sliders open with the wind blowing through indicated she was already gone.

Jacob burst in behind him, and Liam followed, searching the room and master bath.

Fletch hurried onto the deck and scanned the woods. But he didn't see Jane.

"Where the hell did she go?" Jacob asked from behind him.

Fletch shook his head. "She must have panicked when she heard you guys."

"Or she's been lying and using you," Jacob suggested.

No…he couldn't have been a fool. Not again.

Liam shook his head. "Running doesn't look good for her case, Fletch."

His brother didn't have to tell him that. He'd trusted Jane. And he thought she'd trusted him.

He stepped back inside and he checked his pack.

Dammit to hell, she'd stolen his gun.

As THE POLICE car raced up behind Jane, déjà vu struck her. Another time when she'd been chased. Another siren.

No…that didn't seem right…

The car suddenly veered around her. She pressed the brake, preparing to pull over. She was armed, but she didn't intend to shoot a cop.

Instead, though, the officer sped up and shot past her at lightning speed, disappearing around the curve ahead.

Relief whooshed through her chest. She'd lucked out twice now. Her luck wouldn't last forever.

She couldn't keep running, either. But before she saw Fletch again or turned herself in, she wanted to be able to tell him the truth. Everything.

After he'd protected her and saved her life, he deserved it.

Anxious to get this over with, she sped up slightly, maneuvering the curvy road. She passed the cactus rock formation with a shiver.

Why had Halls had that photograph of her and her husband in his briefcase where he kept his files on divorce cases?

The old truck bounced over ruts in the road as she veered down the dirt road to the cabin. The shadows in the trees looked ominous as she drove beneath the canopy of oaks with moss dripping down like dead snakes hanging from the branches. The truck's tires churned through the soggy, snowy ground, sucking at the wet mud and rocks.

Hopefully Halls was long gone, and she'd have time to explore the inside of the cabin alone. A tree branch snapped off under the weight of the melting snow and struck her windshield, and she startled and swerved off the road.

The truck's front rammed into the ditch, and the tires churned at the soggy ground. She flew forward, hands clenching the steering wheel in a white-knuckled grip to brace herself. The steering wheel snapped tight, nearly choking her as the truck lurched to a dead stop.

She pounded the steering wheel, then shifted the truck into Reverse to back up. But mud and gravel spewed as the truck ground itself deeper into the muddy mess.

Realizing she was only making matters worse, Jane cut the engine and leaned her head against the steering wheel to calm herself. She wasn't that far from the cabin.

She'd walk the rest of the way. God knows, she'd hiked her share the past few days. What was another mile or two?

Resigned, she snagged Fletch's gun, tucked it into her jacket pocket, then slid from the pickup. Her boots sucked at the slush, but she climbed back onto the dirt road and began to walk. Sunshine tried to steal its way through the spiny branches of the trees and failed, adding a chill to the air.

Limbs cracked and twigs snapped from the tree branches as she wove around the narrow, winding road. Somewhere in the distance, an animal howled, and a dog barked. Squirrels scampered up the trees and dug in the snow for food. A deer darted past in the woods, startling her, and she automatically put her hand in her pocket to access the gun.

A mile through the forest, and she was almost there. She saw the house on the hill. She froze as she neared, scanning the property for a car in case Halls was there.

The driveway was empty. So was the area to the side of the house.

Breathing easier, she rounded the last curve into the clearing where the house sat. She studied it, hoping for something in her mind to click. The cabin seemed familiar.

Except the house she remembered being at with the man with the tattoo was in a neighborhood. She'd seen other couples, the grill firing up, wine floating…

She had not lived here. That realization was so strong that she forged ahead. If she hadn't shared this house with her husband, why had Halls brought her here and told her she had?

Because something bad had happened here.

Bracing herself for whatever might happen, she took a deep breath and walked up the hill toward the cabin. The house had a chimney. In her mind, she saw a fire burning inside the fireplace.

It seemed cozy. No, not cozy. All wrong.

Heart racing, she passed a wooden wagon that must have been used to house a flower bed, because weeds had overtaken it.

She'd done this before. Walked up to this cabin, knowing something was wrong.

A face appeared in the shadows of her mind. A man's. The man with the tattoo.

Then a voice behind them. "I've been expecting you."

Jane froze as something hard jabbed her lower back.

The voice in her mind. It was the same one speaking now. "I knew you'd come back here. I've just been waiting until you showed."

Images of being shoved in the house at gunpoint blended with reality as the man pushed her up the steps to the porch door.

Chapter Twenty

"She ran, didn't she?" Jacob asked.

Fletch wanted to defend Jane, but the answer to his brother's question was obvious. "She went searching for the truth. I told you she saved my life."

"By shooting a man," Jacob interjected.

Fletch shrugged. "In self-defense."

"She can't get very far on foot," Jacob said. "Which means she may be looking for a car to steal." He snatched his phone. "I'll see if there have been any reports in the last hour." Jacob stepped into the den, then outside on the back deck.

Liam scowled at Fletch. "You mentioned those couples in Jane's nightmare. I want to check something. Your laptop in the den?"

Fletch nodded and motioned for Liam to follow him. He'd left his computer on the small desk in the corner. He retrieved it and carried it to the breakfast bar. While Liam connected to the FBI's database, Fletch brewed another pot of coffee and handed his brother a mug.

Jacob joined them a minute later with a grim look. "Nothing so far. But Deputy Rowan said he'd let me know if anything comes in."

Fletch watched as several pictures appeared on the computer screen. Three different couples, dead, blood pooling around their lifeless bodies.

"This first couple, Deidre and Arnie Richter lived outside Asheville," Liam said. "At first, police thought it was a murder suicide. Wife's throat was slit. Husband died of a gunshot wound to the chest. From interviewing neighbors, we learned the couple was having marital problems. Wife cheated on husband. We suspected he killed her and then turned the weapon on himself."

"Is that what happened?" Fletch asked.

"I'll get to that. But one point that stuck out was that the letter *C* was carved in the palm of the woman's hand. Police speculated *C* for cheater." Liam sighed. "There's more." He scrolled to another set of crime photos. A redheaded woman sprawled on the bed with blood sprayed across the white comforter. A dark-haired man slumped in the chair beside the bed, his body limp, blood soaking his shirt from a gunshot wound to the chest.

"This is Renee and William Purdue," Liam said. "Similar story. Marriage in trouble. Woman was seeing the husband's best friend on the side."

Liam zeroed in on a close-up shot of the woman's hand. "The letter *C* on her hand exactly like the first female victim." Liam looked up at them. "This is when we realized there might be a pattern, that the murder/suicide theory on couple number one might be off base."

"Or the second murders could have been a copycat of the first," Jacob suggested.

"We considered that." Liam scrolled to a third couple. "But meet Bailey and Jim Hearst."

"The same MO," Jacob said.

Liam clicked his mouth. "Exactly. Which suggests that—"

"There's a serial killer murdering couples," Fletch finished.

"That's our theory now," Liam said. "So far the press hasn't gotten hold of this, but we've dubbed him the CK, couples killer."

"Do you think Jane witnessed one of these murders?" Fletch asked. "Or that she knows who the CK is?"

"Considering what you told me about the images of dead couples she remembered, that's a possibility. Or—" he hesitated "—perhaps she and her husband were having marital problems and the CK tried to kill them, but Jane escaped."

Fletch couldn't imagine Jane as the type of woman to cheat on her husband. "If that's true, why didn't he slit her throat the way he did the other women, when he carried her into the woods?"

"Good point." Liam's phone buzzed. "The lab." He connected the call and stepped to the deck again.

Jacob was studying him with a pensive expression. "You really like this woman, don't you?"

Fletch shifted. "I just don't want to see her get hurt."

"Be careful, bro. She may not be the person you think she is."

"So you've told me." Fletch tightened his jaw. How could he argue when there were so many unknowns?

Liam's boots pounded on the floor as he strode back inside. "Talked to the Federal Marshals."

Jacob folded his arms. "And?"

"Jane's not in WITSEC. In fact, it looks like we were wrong about everything about her."

Fletch's stomach knotted. So who was Jane?

JANE TENSED, GRINDING her teeth as Halls shoved her up the steps. Her right hand slid to her pocket to retrieve Fletch's gun, but Halls's sardonic laugh sliced through the air.

"Not going to happen." Instead he jerked her arm out of the way, reached inside and withdrew the weapon.

She silently cursed herself for walking into an ambush. He pushed her forward so hard she had to grab the doorjamb to keep from hitting the floor on her knees.

"I thought your amnesia was a blessing and decided I might just let you live, but then you hooked up with that damn cop's brother, and I knew it was only a matter of time before you figured out the truth."

Only she hadn't.

She scanned the property as she stumbled toward the front door. The area was surrounded by thick, tall trees. Shadows clung to the walls of the dark interior as she entered. She stumbled, the room swaying as the scent of blood and death assaulted her.

Foul odors wafted from the hallway to the right. She rounded the corner and saw the fireplace.

But her vision blurred and she saw blood spatter dotting the stone.

Then blood spatter on the floor and walls, on her hands and clothes.

She slowly pivoted to stare at him. "You killed him."

"Yes, Jade, I had to. The two of you were getting too close to the truth."

Jade, not Jane? Reality hacked at the frayed edges of her mind. Jade…that was her name.

Jade Jenkins.

Her husband's face looked back at her, ghost-like and eerie.

She saw him sliding the wedding ring on her finger, their heads bent in hushed whispers as they made plans.

They were in an office with a whiteboard on the wall. A whiteboard full of pictures of dead people. Three different married couples, the women's throats brutally slashed, pale skin bloody, eyes wide open in the shock of death.

Then the men, their husbands. In close proximity to the women's bodies, as if they'd been staged. A female hand reaching for help from her loved one. Or vice versa.

But their hands couldn't touch. The letter C was carved on the women's palms. Symbolic.

A gaping hole in the men's chests, blood-soaked shirts shredded by the impact of the bullet.

Three murders with the same MO. A serial killer was targeting couples. They'd dubbed him the CK, couples killer.

He had to be stopped before he took more lives.

She and Louie hadn't been married. She was a detective and Louie was her partner. They'd gone undercover as husband and wife to sniff out the killer.

The cookout in the neighborhood, the wine and her interior design business—all part of the undercover story. She'd chosen that career because her mother was a designer and she knew enough about the business and lingo to fake it.

The neighborhood had been in the targeted

area. She and Louie infiltrated the close-knit group because they suspected the CK was friends with at least one of the couples.

That they'd met him when seeking a divorce attorney.

She and Louie were onto him. And when he'd invited them to his house to discuss their proposed divorce, they'd come. Prepared. At least they thought they were.

But Halls had made them for cops. They'd barely walked through the door when he slammed the butt of his gun against her temple. She'd swayed and stars danced behind her eyes as she grappled for control.

Low, muffled voices echoed through the fog... Louie's. Halls's.

Halls had slashed the women's throats while the husbands watched as a form of punishment.

Jade struggled to reach her weapon, but Louie opened fire on Halls. Halls ducked aside and fired, shooting Louie in the heart. Blood gushed from his chest, and his body bounced backward. His gun hit the floor. She scrambled on her hands and knees to reach it. She picked it up to shoot Halls, but he grabbed her hair and jerked her head backward. Then the knife...the sharp blade coming toward her.

She threw her arm up to deflect the blade, but Halls bellowed, jammed the knife in his pocket and used the gun instead. This time the blow was *so hard and swift and violent that the world tilted and went dark.*

Sometime later, she came to and found herself in a dark cave. She was tied and gagged. It was pitch-dark, and snow was falling. Then she heard footsteps. She struggled to untie herself. Had to hurry. Finally the knot slipped free. She lurched up to run, had to get away from him.

He hadn't slit her throat and left her with Louie because he didn't want their deaths to be labeled CK kills. But he was going to kill her. Out here in the middle of nowhere, where the animals could ravage her body and destroy any evidence he might have left.

SHE BLINKED BACK into focus. Woodruff Halls, attorney at law.

"You are the CK," she said. "My partner and I figured it out."

Halls was a chameleon. His handsome, polished smile could be charming at times. But he morphed into a demented monster in a flash. His skin looked sallow and his eyes bulged, creating deep, dark ugly pockets.

"Yes," he said in a menacing tone, "and this time you're going to die, and no one will ever find you."

FLETCH SHIFTED ONTO the balls of his feet. "Don't drag it out, Liam. Who is she?"

"Detective Jade Jenkins," Liam said.

"Jane is a police officer?" Fletch's mind raced. Her ability to fight, shoot…it made sense.

"That's right," Liam replied. "She and her partner Detective Louie Germaine were working the couples killer case. I spoke to her commander myself. According to him, Detective Jenkins and Detective Germaine went undercover as a married couple named Bianca and Victor Renard to trap the CK."

"That's the reason they didn't show up in WIT-SEC," Jacob said.

"And the reason for the fake identities and story about the real estate agency," Fletch added.

Liam nodded. "Acting as a real estate agency with interior design services allowed them access to people's homes where they could meet the neighbors and couples in the community."

Liam's news echoed in Fletch's ears. Jane and her partner went undercover. She was never married. *Never* married…

"Her partner was killed?" Fletch asked.

"Yes, shot in the chest like the other male victims of the CK. My guess is Jade and Germaine determined the killer's identity, and he realized they were onto him, so he had to shut them up."

"So he shoots the male partner and takes Jade into the woods to kill her," Jacob filled in. "Leaving her with her partner and using the same MO would have pointed to the CK."

"Instead, he planned to frame Jane, I mean Jade, for her partner's death," Fletch said.

Jacob crossed his arms. "Then he used Officer Clemmens to plant evidence and lead us astray."

"Dammit, and I let her leave with Halls that day," Jacob muttered.

"Don't beat yourself up," Liam said. "Halls looked legit. But one of our techs dug deeper into the lawyer. He and his wife divorced about six weeks ago."

Jacob's brows shot up. "About the same time as the CK started?"

"Exactly," Liam said. "We're obtaining search warrants for his home and office."

"You think Halls is the CK?" Fletch asked, piecing everything together.

"Everything's pointing that way." Liam jangled his keys. "I'm going to his home to search." He gave Jacob a pointed look. "It'll be faster if we divide up. You take his office."

"Will do."

"Damn, Halls might already have Jade, and he's hell bent on silencing her." Fletch stepped forward to follow Liam.

"Then stay here in case she calls you or comes back," Jacob said.

Fletch scrubbed his hand over his face, panic threatening. "I can't lose her," he muttered before he even realized what he'd said.

"Then let us do our jobs," Liam said quietly. "We'll find her, Fletch."

He hoped to hell Liam was right. "At least leave the files open about the case. I'll search through them and see if anything sticks out. Maybe another property Halls owns, some place he might take Jade."

He ushered his brothers out the door. They had to hurry.

Chapter Twenty-One

Fletch pulled up everything he could find on Detective Jade Jenkins from the databases Liam had accessed on his computer.

Jade was thirty-two years old, had studied criminology and behavioral science before attending the police academy. She worked as a beat cop in Asheville for four years before becoming a detective, first in the robbery unit, then homicide.

The photograph of her receiving a commendation for saving a child from a cold-blooded killer, aka the child's father, stirred his admiration.

He had been right about her. Jade wasn't a killer. She risked her life to save others on a daily basis.

He searched deeper and found information about her family. Born to Mildred and Herman Jenkins, she was an only child whose father was a judge. Her mother was an interior decorator. Probably the reason she'd used a design career as her cover story.

A reporter named Lynn Wellman had covered

the couple's murder and included family photographs of the couple together with Jade as a child. One picture showed her sitting on her father's lap, doing the Sunday crossword puzzle just as she'd described.

He skimmed for details of their murder. According to the investigating officer, Detective Roger Stint, the couple had been killed in what first appeared to be a home invasion. The fact that the wife's expensive jewelry and silver hadn't been stolen, though, indicated robbery wasn't the motive. The judge's safe had been opened, yet cash left inside.

The judge's secretary stated that Judge Jenkins often carried photocopies of important documents and files home to review, and that he kept those in a home safe. The fact that he'd sentenced numerous convicted felons to prison opened up a wide suspect pool.

Persons of interest in the case included a gang member who'd been sentenced to life. However, police couldn't prove gang involvement. Another suspect was the father of a convicted rapist who insisted the girl got what she deserved.

Scumbag.

But the father had a rock-solid alibi for the time of the double homicide.

Later, the crime team matched a partial fingerprint lifted from the back door to a man named Otis Rigley, who was then being tried for his wife's murder. Rigley had a list of arrests a mile long. He'd killed the Jenkins couple so the judge's death would cause a mistrial. While awaiting a new trial, Rigley was out on bond. Then he'd suddenly disappeared.

Finally, the following June, he was stopped on a routine traffic violation. The officer ran his name and realized he'd skipped bail. So Rigley was arrested and this time convicted.

After serving twenty years of his life sentence, he had been paroled just a month ago.

Fletch tensed. Rigley was the man Jade had shot. The man who'd shot him.

Fletch drummed his fingers on the counter. As a lawyer, Halls had connections to police officers, parole officers, PIs, and inmates and ex-cons.

What if Halls had arranged for early parole for Rigley, then hired him to kill Jane?

Jane's—Jade's—face flashed in Fletch's mind. Jade as the little girl whose parents had been brutally killed in her own home. Jade hearing the gunshots and her mother's screams.

Jade discovering their bodies and calling 911 the next morning.

She'd been sent to live with her grandmother, but lost her at age nineteen.

Then she'd been truly alone.

A hollow ache dug at his gut.

Now she was alone out there again. Looking

for the truth. Justice. Battling a ruthless killer who wanted her dead.

Her job as a cop explained her toughness. And her instincts that Halls couldn't be trusted.

But she was still vulnerable, and a serial killer was after her. A serial killer who looked normal. One who no one would suspect if they saw him with Jade.

FEAR TWISTED JADE'S gut inside out, but she fought its vile clutches. She would not give in to fear. And she would not die at this madman's hands.

He had killed Louie. Her partner. Her friend.

Along with six other people so far.

Seven if the vile smell emanating from the house was what she suspected.

"So," she said, determined to get him to spill his guts before he did hers. "You discovered your wife was cheating on you and that made you angry." She offered him a sardonic smile. "What happened? Did your long hours get to her? Didn't you give her enough attention? Or was she just a whore who became bored and liked to sleep around?"

Rage flared in his eyes and he drew back his hand and slapped her across the cheek. The sting smarted, but she clenched her teeth to keep from crying out.

The last time they'd fought, he'd won. Today the outcome was going to be different. It had to be.

"I did not neglect that woman," Halls said bitterly. "I gave her everything. A beautiful home, fancy clothes, expensive jewelry and elaborate vacations. But she didn't appreciate my hard work."

"No, she didn't," Jade said, playing along. She had to stall. "She took you for granted, enjoyed the nice things you gave her. Then she was selfish and wanted more, didn't she?"

"Exactly," he snarled as he waved his gun in front of her face. "Just like those other bitches. Their stupid, pathetic husbands were like me. They sacrificed their time and worked hard to provide, but their wives were spoiled and demanded more and more."

"After a while, nothing you did was enough," Jade guessed. "The country club dinners and wine and parties weren't exciting anymore. So your wife went looking for fun on the side."

Halls began to pace, his features lined with agitation, his movements jerky. "She did. After all I sacrificed to make her happy, she was an ungrateful bitch." He paused and stared at her, anger oozing from his pores. "I even gave up criminal work and accepted divorce cases to have more time for her. And then she lied to me, just like all women lie." He waved the gun toward her. "That's one thing my job taught me. You can't trust anyone in a skirt."

Jade resisted the urge to snap at him for his

sexist remark. "I'm not a liar," she said. "If I was married, I would never cheat on my husband."

"Hell, you're the worst kind," Halls shouted. "You lied about being married! I watched you play the part in front of all those other couples." He gripped her arm, fingers digging into her skin painfully. "You're so good at it, you fooled them all. Because that's what you do. You lie to get what you want. You entrap people with your lies. You lie to suspects and even to the victims when you tell them everything will be okay." He shook her. "But nothing is okay when you're lied to."

Jade forced her voice to remain calm as she mentally struggled to formulate a plan. She was a detective, she knew how to do that.

And she and Louie had narrowed the suspects down to focus on Halls.

What else did she know about him?

He dragged her toward the back of the house down the hallway. The stench of death grew stronger, nauseating, permeating the air.

"You don't have to do this," she said. "You've punished your wife. She paid for her sins."

"And you're going to pay for yours."

FLETCH HAD BEEN pacing for over an hour, but still no word from his brothers or Jade.

Dammit, he was about to lose his mind.

He snatched his keys to start hunting but realized that would be foolish. He had no idea where she'd gone.

Or where to find Halls.

His phone buzzed, and he lurched toward the bar to answer it. Jacob.

Please, dear God. Let it be good news. Please let his brother be calling to say they'd found Halls and arrested him. And that Jade was alive.

His pulse hammered as he connected the call. "Jacob?"

"Yeah. You're on speaker with me and Liam."

Fletch released a ragged breath. "What did you find?"

"Sorry, we haven't found her yet," Liam said. "But we may be getting closer."

Fletch stepped onto the back deck and stared into the thick pockets of woods. He'd met Jade in a blizzard and they'd both nearly died. But they had survived.

She had to survive this time.

"Go on," he said through clenched teeth.

Jacob spoke first. "A report just came in. Stolen pickup truck a few miles from your cabin. Gray, rusted out, nineteen eighty model." He recited the license plate.

"Did the owner see who stole it?" Fletch asked.

"No, it was parked by his barn near the road. A BOLO has been issued. Truck was spotted due north about a half hour ago."

Fletch racked his brain. He knew the area.

Countryside. Farms. Roads weaving past small towns as they snaked up the mountains.

"Could be teenagers," Jacob said.

Fletch ran a hand through his hair. He had a feeling. "It's her."

"Where the hell is she going?" Liam asked.

Fear clawed at Fletch as the truth dawned. "Back to that cabin where Halls took her. She wants answers and is going after them herself."

Alone. With no backup.

Dammit, he had to find her. "I've looked for other properties Halls owns but had no luck. Did you find something?"

"A crime team is going over his house from top to bottom. So far, nothing about another property or anything pointing to him as the CK."

Jacob cut in, "Halls's secretary has been helpful. Said Halls used to be calm, orderly, good with clients, meticulous with the details of his cases. But when he discovered his wife was cheating on him, he started acting differently." Jacob paused. "He became enraged for his clients, sympathized with husbands claiming infidelity on their wives' parts."

"Fits with the CK's MO, the *C* carved on the women's palms," Liam said.

"Right." Jacob heaved a breath. "I did find a link to the PI. Odd thing is that he didn't work for Halls. He was working for the daughter of one of Halls's victims. He was on Halls's scent. So Halls either killed him or had him killed."

Fletch filled them in on what he'd learned about the Jenkins's double murder. "Rigley was sent to finish Jade. He probably killed the PI as well, because he was getting too close to the truth."

"That fits. I'm alerting all law enforcement agencies to look for Halls," Liam said. "As of today, he's on our Most Wanted list."

Jacob cleared his throat. "Now we just have to figure out where he's going."

Fletch worked Search and Rescue. He knew the mountains. The trail.

"Let me know if you find an address for a second property."

"Copy that. I'll look into the wife and her family. Property might be under her name." Jacob disconnected, and Fletch walked over to the corkboard above his desk and studied the map on the wall.

He inserted a pushpin at his location, then another at the address where the truck was stolen, and analyzed the roads in the area.

Halls might take Jade to a second home if he had one. Or…in desperation, he might kill her and dump her on the side of the road or off the mountain. Somewhere no one would ever find her.

God… He pinched the bridge of his nose. He couldn't let that happen.

Chapter Twenty-Two

Fletch's keys jangled in his hand as he scribbled a note to Jade telling her he was looking for her, that if she showed up, to hide in his house and call him.

But he couldn't just sit around and do nothing. He wanted to be nearer where that truck was last spotted, in case Jacob or Liam learned a location for a second property or Jade was seen by the police.

He spread his map on the console. He knew these mountains better than anyone and had a good idea where that truck was heading. At least the general direction. There were hundreds of cabins tucked away to the northeast of Whistler, where skiing and whitewater rafting were popular.

That cactus-shaped formation of rocks seemed familiar.

He relied on his built-in GPS to showcase the roads as he drove. Impatience nagged at him as he encountered traffic, and he maneuvered around a minivan and a pickup carrying farm supplies. Two teens on motor scooters sped down the shoulder of the road, weaving in and out of traffic, on a joyride.

Once upon a time, he and his brothers had been daredevils, too. Truthfully, he still was, to a degree.

But losing both parents so quickly had taught him how precious life could be. That a loved one could be swiped from you in a second.

Jane's face flashed behind his eyes. Jade—not Jane.

Jade…a loved one?

Hell, he knew he cared about her. And the idea of losing her terrified him.

JADE SWALLOWED BACK bile at the strong odor of blood and death permeating the walls of the cabin.

Her ears were ringing where Halls had slammed her head against the hard wall.

"She's here, isn't she?" Jade rasped.

A maniacal laugh punctuated the air. "Who?"

"Your wife," Jade said, memories beginning to slip through her foggy mind as her vision cleared. "She cheated on you, so you killed her."

"She deserved it, the ungrateful bitch. I took her to Tahiti!"

He was escalating. Jade had to keep him talking, buy some more time. "That sounds romantic," she said. "You planned a special trip for her."

Another sarcastic bark of a laugh. "She used me to pay for spa treatments and massages, and then, while we were on a midnight cruise, I found texts on her phone from another man. Not just texts," he said shrilly. "Naughty texts. She suggested kinky stuff she never wanted to do with me."

Ah, his ego was bruised. "That was a terrible way to learn she was unfaithful," Jade said.

His eyes flared with rage. "When I asked her about it, she didn't even bother to deny it. She had the gall to tell me about him, how I didn't satisfy her anymore, that she needed a young stud."

"I'm sorry that happened to you." Jade scanned the room for something to use as a weapon. He'd set her gun on the end table in front of the fireplace, out of reach.

"I'm sure you suggested couples counseling, didn't you?" Jade asked. "Told her you wanted to save your marriage."

The whites of his eyes bulged as he glowered at her. "Hell, no, I didn't offer to see a damn shrink. She was the one with the problem, not me!"

"So you decided to get revenge," Jade said quietly.

"I decided she had to pay and she had to suffer," he bellowed. "And she did. I held her down and sliced her neck and laughed as the blood spewed and ran down her pale white throat."

He was mentally ill. Jade remembered now. At one of the dinner parties with the neighbors, she'd seen this strange look in his eyes when he'd watched the women. It had been her first inkling that she and Louie were on the right track. After that, they'd started digging deeper into Woodruff Halls.

Louie... Her heart gave a pang of regret and sadness. They'd been partners for two years, had been friends. He'd taught her how to read people, study body language and identify the little nuances that were some people's tells.

Woodruff had one. When he lied, his right eye twitched slightly. Subtle, but once she'd noticed it and tested him, it had been evident.

That and his temper and underlying bitterness toward women.

He'd passed out his business cards to the neighborhood men like candy to children. More than once she'd overheard him regaling a sordid tale about a cheating spouse.

"I understand why you killed your wife," Jade said calmly. "She hurt you and deserved to be punished."

"She did." His voice cracked.

"But I don't understand why you killed the other couples. They did nothing to you."

He tunneled his fingers through his hair, spiking it until it stood on end. Sweat trickled down the side of his face. "Do you know what it was like listening to my clients blather on and on about their cheating spouses? It was like mine was carving the knife deep in my gut and twisting it."

"That's the reason you carved the letter *C* in your victims' hands."

"You got that right."

"Maybe those women lied to their husbands, but you don't know what went on behind closed doors."

"You think betraying their vows is justified!" He lunged at her, and she pressed a hand to his chest.

"That's not what I mean. But those women weren't totally bad," Jade said. "Deidre Richter had a three-year-old child. She loved her little boy. I saw pictures of them at the park. She volunteered at his preschool. Now that sweet little boy will grow up without a mother." She paused. "And a father. Because you stole his parents from him." She summoned her strength, had to find a way to get that gun from him or reach her own. "That's where I'm confused, Woodruff. I can call you by your first name, can't I?"

Rule number one in negotiation—get personal with the perp. Make them see you as human, and humanize them.

She needed to defuse the situation. Give herself time to retrieve her weapon.

"I…guess so," he stammered, although he looked confused by the request.

"Good, your name is so distinguished." She slowly pushed herself up from the floor. He shot her a warning look and stepped forward, the gun wavering in his trembling hand.

"I just needed to stand up for a minute," she said. "For us to talk face-to-face."

A sneer twisted his mouth. "I watched you with your so-called husband, and I knew you were just like all the others. I could tell you didn't really love him, that it was an act."

Because they hadn't been married. They'd been working undercover.

"Why did you kill the husbands?" she asked. "Can you explain that to me?"

He began to pace again, gun hand flinging out in a wide arc. "Because those idiots came to me whining. Whining and wanting revenge against their wives for being so sorry. But then they started wimping out and begging the stupid whoring women to take them back." His boots clicked on the wood floor, the old boards squeaking. "That bitch Renee slept with her husband's best friend, and William actually wanted to forgive them. Can you believe that?"

"Maybe he didn't want anger to destroy his life."

"He wasn't a real man. None of them were!"

"So you shot them in the heart because their wives broke their hearts, then you killed them because they—"

"Because they should have punished their wives like I did mine!" He turned and aimed the gun at her chest, his lips twisting again. "Just like I'm going to take care of you."

FLETCH FELT LIKE a crazy man as he headed farther up the mountain. The images of what could be happening to Jade taunted him.

Halls had proven he was not only violent, but that he was sadistic. Carving the letter *C* into the women's palms was meant to inflict pain and to mark them like the letter *S* had in *The Scarlet Letter*. Slitting their throats had signified personal rage. And the fact that he'd killed multiple victims meant the murders were not only premeditated, but that he enjoyed the thrill of the kill.

Fletch's phone buzzed as he rounded a curve. Liam. He quickly connected.

"Fletch, any word from Jade?"

"No. Do you have information?"

"One of our analysts dug deep into Woodruff Halls. Apparently his wife divorced him. We tried to reach her, but no one has seen or heard from her in weeks."

Knots of tension coiled inside Fletch's stomach. "Do you think he killed her?"

"That would be my guess. According to a friend of hers, she had an affair. When Halls found out, he went ballistic. She moved to get away from him, but he may have found her."

"She was his trigger, his first kill," Fletch said. "Then he got a taste of blood and decided other cheating wives should suffer."

"That theory fits," Liam said. "As a divorce attorney, he was privy to his clients' personal information. The question is—what did he do with his wife's body?"

An icy chill raced through Fletch's veins. "He could have buried her or hidden her in the mountains."

"Hang on, a text is coming through." A pause, then Liam returned on the line. "Okay, we may have something. Halls's wife's family owned a cabin in a remote section of the mountain. It's possible he killed his wife there."

Fletch's pulse thundered. "That's where he took Jade."

"I'm a half hour away," Liam said.

"Text me the coordinates," Fletch said. "I'm closer."

Liam cursed. "Fletch, this guy is dangerous. He's already killed several people."

"Exactly the reason we can't waste time," Fletch said. "Send me the damn coordinates."

A heartbeat of silence. "All right. But Jacob should be there around the time you arrive. If she's at the cabin or if Halls is, hang back until Jacob arrives."

Fletch mumbled that he would, although he had no intention of waiting.

If Jade was with this maniac, he'd do whatever necessary to save her.

JADE LIFTED HER chin in a show of courage. She was a trained detective. She wouldn't go down without a fight. "Killing me won't serve any purpose," she said. "The police know who you are. They'll find you and you'll go to prison anyway."

"Then I have nothing to lose by adding another body to the count."

"Killing a cop will definitely earn you life without parole. Besides, I don't fit the profile of your other victims. The reason you started killing in the first place."

"Ah, but you've given me another reason," he said with a sinister smile.

His hand trembled. He was rattled, off his game. He'd obviously caught the other couples off guard. Planned the murders and how best to execute them. Details of the crime reports registered in her head. There had been evidence of alcohol in the victims' systems.

She was a loose end he needed to take care of. "Because I'm exposing you as the monster you are." It was now or never. She lunged toward him and he swung the gun toward her and fired.

She dodged the bullet, moved her arm upward and knocked the gun from his hand. It skittered across the floor, and she threw him to the ground. He raised his fist and punched her in the jaw.

Pain knifed through her cheek, and her head spun. Determined not to let him win this fight, she shoved her fist into his belly. He grunted, caught her hair and yanked her head backward. She ground her teeth and tried to jab him in the eyes with her fingers but missed. They traded blows, and she connected with his nose. Blood spurted, and he pressed his hands to his face with a howl.

She took advantage of the moment and scrambled toward his gun.

He bellowed like a crazed animal, then grabbed her leg and yanked her so hard she collapsed onto her stomach. Before she could recover, he kicked her in the lower back sending sharp mind-numbing pain through her extremities. Then he climbed on her back and she suddenly felt the sharp point of a knife at her throat.

"Move, and it's over," he growled.

Jade went still, breath puffing out, anger searing her veins. He climbed off her, snagged the gun and dragged her to her feet. The barrel of the weapon dug into her back.

"Come on, since you've been so chatty, I'm going to satisfy your curiosity before I kill you."

She channeled her anger into a lethal calm.

But he pressed the gun to her head and pushed her down the steps. She grasped the stair rail to keep from tumbling into the darkness, and he clenched her arm and hauled her over the steps and across a concrete floor.

The odor grew stronger, sickening decay at its worst.

Then he shoved her up against an old freezer, opened it and forced her to look inside.

"See, that's where you're going now."

She clawed at the edge of the freezer edge to escape. This man was much more disturbed than she'd imagined.

He'd enjoyed killing his wife so much he hadn't disposed of her body. Instead he'd kept it as a trophy and watched it rot.

"I used to think she was beautiful," he said in a sick voice, as if he was far away, lost in a memory. "But cheating made her ugly. And now look at her."

A sinister laugh echoed off the walls in the cold dank basement, then he lifted the lid of the second freezer.

Terror swept through Jade.

She threw her elbow back and slammed it into his chest, then swung around to fight. But he was too fast.

He whacked the butt of the gun against her temple, and the world spun out of control. She struggled and clawed at him, at the freezer edge to keep from falling inside.

But he hit her again with such force that she tumbled into the darkness.

Chapter Twenty-Three

Jade roused from unconsciousness to a cloying odor. The air felt stale and she couldn't breathe. She tried to move, but her hand made contact with a wall.

The freezer! Oh, God, he'd locked her in the freezer and left her to suffocate to death.

No air. And it was hot. She wouldn't freeze to death, but unless she found a way out, she would die.

No...she couldn't die. She'd just finally remembered who she was, how her partner had died. The reason she'd jumped at the assignment to go undercover and capture the CK. Her parents had been victims. Not related cases, but seeing a wife and husband lying dead together had triggered the trauma of her past. Because of that, she'd volunteered for the undercover assignment to catch the CK.

And the man in the woods who'd come after her...the one she'd shot...she suddenly remembered why he seemed familiar. He'd been serving time in prison for her parents' murder. Woodruff Halls had taken advantage of that fact. Hired him to come after her. Probably told the man that she remembered him.

Knew that seeing him would add to her trauma.

No wonder she'd repressed her memories.

She inhaled shallow breaths to conserve air as she clawed at the top of the freezer. She pushed and shoved, then raked her fingers along the inside, searching for a release latch.

Finally she found one, but when she twisted at the latch, nothing happened. She struggled with it again, and the heavy lid slipped slightly, but refused to budge. A clanging sound echoed from above.

Dear God, the maniac had locked the freezer shut with a chain lock.

Tears pooled in her eyes as terror gripped her. How had she let him get the drop on her?

She blinked back tears, her chest aching with regret. If she didn't find a way out of here, she would die.

Fletch and his brothers might eventually figure out the truth about Halls and find her body.

But Fletch would never know how she felt about him.

For years, she'd been driven by the need to obtain justice for others who'd suffered the loss of a family member as she had. She'd been so focused on the job she'd avoided getting close to anyone.

It hurt too much to lose someone. It was better not to care. Not to dream about love or marriage or children.

But now in what might be the final moments of her life, that was all she could think about.

A life with love. Maybe a wedding and babies. A family that she hadn't had in a really long time.

A family with Fletch that she might never have.

FLETCH RACED AROUND a curve, brakes squealing as he sped up the graveled road to the address Liam had sent.

Sludge left from the snowstorm spewed from his tires, mud and ice spraying. He accelerated and bounced over the ruts, then spotted the small cabin set off the road with the mountains rising behind it.

He searched for Halls's Cadillac, but he didn't see it. He didn't see the truck Jane had stolen, either. Although Halls could have hidden a vehicle or the truck in the woods nearby.

Adrenaline pumped through him. Jacob was close, but he couldn't sit and wait. If Halls was holding Jade here, there was no telling what he might be doing to her.

Jade was strong, experienced, could fight and

shoot. But Halls could have ambushed her and she might be at his mercy right now.

It took only seconds to kill someone. The bastard had slit the other women's throats.

Fear choked him as a dark image filled his mind. No…he couldn't let Jade die like that. He hadn't even told her he loved her.

And he did love her, dammit.

He swung his vehicle to the side of the road a few hundred feet from the clearing, wishing he had his gun. No time to waste, though. Jade's life depended on his quick action.

He slid from his Jeep, eased the door closed, then slowly wove behind the trees flanking the drive toward the cabin.

He scanned the front yard and surrounding property for signs of Halls or Jade. The place seemed eerily quiet, though. Dark inside. No movement. No noise. No signs anyone was here.

Heart hammering, he crossed the distance, ducking and keeping low until he reached the house. He peeked inside the side window at the living room. Empty.

He kept low and moved around the back of the cabin, then peered through another door. Laundry room. Dark. No one inside.

He continued to scope out the property as he inched around to the rear of the cabin. A small deck backed up to what appeared to be a sunroom. All glass along the back. No one visible.

He walked around the far corner and came to another window. This time when he looked inside, he saw a shadow. His breath stalled in his chest as he eased a fraction of an inch closer for a better view of the room in its entirety.

He didn't see Jade. But Halls sat at a desk flipping through a photo album. The hair on the back of his neck bristled at the sinister leer on the man's face. Fletch gritted his teeth and stood on tiptoe to see what he was looking at.

He choked back revulsion when he saw the macabre snapshots. Photos of Halls's victims.

The wind picked up suddenly, rattling the windowpane, and Halls jerked his gaze toward the window. Fletch ducked. But dammit, Halls had seen him.

Hoping the man wasn't armed, Fletch circled to the back deck, then started to climb the stairs. Before he reached the door, it swung open and a gunshot blasted the air.

Fletch dodged the bullet and jumped behind the railing for cover just as Halls barreled down the steps and opened fire. Then Halls darted to the right and ran around the side of the cabin. Fletch chased him, but Halls shot at him again, and he had to seek cover behind a tree.

The man raced down the hill, and Fletch spotted a compact sedan parked beneath a cluster of trees, hidden by the gnarled branches.

Halls jumped inside the vehicle and started the

engine. Fletch dashed toward the car, but Halls fired at him again through the open window. Then Halls accelerated and spun around in the driveway, slinging gravel.

Mud and snowy slush spewed from the back of the car as Halls tore down the drive.

Fletch knotted his hands into fists as he started toward his Jeep. He could go after him. But he wasn't armed.

And if Jade was inside, she needed him. Every second counted.

He punched Jacob's number, his chest heaving for breath as he ran back to the cabin.

"I'm almost there," Jacob said.

"Halls was here. Fired at me and just escaped in a compact dark green sedan." He recited the man's license plate.

"On it."

"I'm going inside to search for Jade."

"Copy that."

Jacob's siren wailed. He *was* near. Maybe he could catch the bastard.

Fear drove him into the house, and he combed the living room. "Jade? Are you here?"

No sound except for his boots pounding the rustic wooden floor. "Jade, where are you?"

He continued to shout her name as he strode through each room, searching closets and cabinets and beneath the beds. No Jade. Dammit, where was she? Was she even here?

He finished searching the kitchen, then the pantry, then walked through the house again, flipping on lights this time. A terrible stench hit him. Blood? Death?

He followed the source and found a doorway in the hall. He'd missed it in his haste to search the rooms.

He turned the knob, but it was locked. Palms sweating, he jiggled it over and over, but the door refused to budge. He shined his pin light on the lock and realized it was the old-fashioned kind that required a key.

Halls probably had the damn thing with him. He checked the kitchen drawers and cabinets and the desk in the bedroom. The photo album of Halls's victims mocked him. Dear God, he didn't want to see Jade's picture among those faces.

He searched the top of the desk, the shelf above it, then the drawer. No key.

Cursing, he raced outside to his car and retrieved the lock-picking tool set he kept in the trunk. He hurried back into the house with it and darted straight to the door. Dropping to his knees, he jammed the small tool into the keyhole opening and wiggled it until the lock clicked free.

Nerves crawled along his spine as he jerked the door open. Darkness bathed the basement. That horrible, acrid odor assaulted him. Worse down there.

Please, God, no… "Jade!" Nothing.

He raced down the wooden steps. The stench grew stronger, vile in its intensity. Someone had died here.

Jade?

Nausea threatened, but he swallowed it down and scanned the dank interior. A couple of garbage bags in the corner. Two compact freezers.

He darted over to the garbage bags first. Holding his breath, he untied the bags and looked inside. Relief came momentarily. Just trash.

But the freezers... The odor was coming from there.

"Jade!" He shouted her name over and over as he crossed the room to the first one. Both were locked with padlock chains.

Dread curled through every cell in his body. No time to waste. He scanned the basement until he located a storage closet. He ran to it, ripped open the door and found bolt cutters inside.

Shaking with fear, he hurried back and opened the first freezer. The raunchy smell of decay assaulted him the moment he lifted the lid. Then horror. A dead woman inside. Her body in serious stages of decomposition. Eyes blank, inside deep hollow sockets where skin and bone had rotted.

He shoved the door shut, leaned back and exhaled, forcing himself to focus. He couldn't vomit now. Had to find Jade.

Cold terror gripped him as he cut the chain on the other freezer. "Jade!"

Praying she was still alive, he lifted the lid.

God help him… Jade lay curled inside, un-conscious.

Chapter Twenty-Four

Fletch called Jade's name again, but she didn't move. Fear pulsed through him, and he leaned over the freezer and lifted her from the inside. She was limp, her face bruised.

But thank God, Halls hadn't slit her throat.

Still, what had he done to her?

He carried her up the steps into the den and laid her on the couch, then checked for a pulse. Barely discernible.

But she was alive.

"Jade, I'm here. Help is on the way." He quickly checked her body for visible injuries. Cut marks from a knife—no. Bruises—yes. Another blow to the head—yes.

He punched 911 on his phone, gave the operator the address and described Jade's condition. "Hurry," he finished. "Please hurry!"

Footsteps sounded outside, and he jumped up and checked the window. Relief hit him.

Liam.

He yanked open the front door. "I found Jade," Fletch stammered. "And called an ambulance."

Liam grimaced. "The smell?"

"A body downstairs."

"Probably Halls's wife," Liam said. "No one has seen her in weeks. I'll get the ME and a CSI team out here ASAP. Jacob issued a full-scale hunt for Halls."

Fletch wanted to hear that the man was caught. Or dead. Not that he was still on the loose. Still a threat to Jade.

"We'll catch him," Liam assured him.

Fletch darted back to Jade while Liam made the call for the evidence recovery team and ME. She still lay unconscious, breath shallow, complexion pasty white. He dropped onto the sofa beside her and cradled her hand in his. "Jade, an ambulance is on the way." She didn't respond, intensifying his anxiety. He gestured toward the hallway as Liam ended the call.

"There's evidence in the bedroom, too," Fletch said. "Halls kept a photo album with pictures of his victims."

"His souvenirs. Sick bastard," Liam muttered.

"Yeah, and he has to pay." Fletch gently brushed a strand of hair from Jade's face. "Hang on," Fletch whispered. "Just hang on, darlin'."

JADE STIRRED FROM unconsciousness and gasped. A male voice, gruff and concerned, floated to her through the darkness.

The last thing she remembered was being knocked over the head and shoved into a freezer. She gasped again. She was suffocating. Lost in the darkness. She was going to die.

"Jade, it's okay, you're in the hospital now."

The voice, gruff, worried, tender… Fletch.

She opened her eyes and couldn't believe she was looking at him. "Fletch?"

A smile flickered onto his face. "Yeah, I'm here."

Confusion muddled her mind, then a shiver rippled through her as she relived the horror of seeing Halls's dead wife in that freezer.

"He killed his wife," she said in a low whisper.

Fletch stroked her hair from her forehead. "I know, I found her body just before I found you." He lowered his head and laid it against her chest for a moment, then lifted it again. "God, Jade, I was afraid I'd find you the same way."

It was her turn to smile. She threaded her fingers in his hair, so grateful to see him that her chest ached. "No, not me. You know I'm tough."

He chuckled. "Still, you had me worried. You shouldn't have gone off alone."

She licked her dry lips. "I didn't want to cause problems between you and your brothers. I know how much they mean to you."

His breath rattled out, then he kissed her hand. "You mean a lot to me, too, Jade."

Her eyes flickered with surprise. "You know my name?"

He nodded. She longed to tell him that she loved him. But that wouldn't be fair, not when he didn't know the real Jade. "I remember now. I know what happened."

He kissed her hand again. "I know who you are, about your undercover work."

Her heart fluttered. "You do?"

He nodded, eyes searching hers. "Tell me what you remember."

"Everything," she said. "When Halls took me into that house, it all came rushing back. He was the couples killer. My partner, Louie, and I were undercover in that neighborhood to catch him."

"And Halls made you two as detectives," Fletch said.

She nodded. "Louie… He took a bullet to save me."

Fletch gripped her hand. "Were you two…involved?"

Tears threatened. "No, just good friends and partners. He taught me a lot about detective work."

Fletch nodded. "What do you remember about your personal life? Do you have someone special waiting for you?"

"You mean, do I have a boyfriend?" she said softly.

Fletch shrugged, but before she could answer, his brothers Liam and Jacob rapped on the door and stuck their heads in.

Jade clenched the sheets. "Did you catch Halls?"

FLETCH WANTED THE answer to his question to Jade. But first, he needed to know if Halls was in custody.

"Our agents caught up with him at the airport," Liam said. "He was about to fly to South America."

"So he's in custody?" Fletch asked.

"Yes," Liam said. "Thanks to you, Jade, and you, Fletch, for the evidence you collected, that bastard is going away for a long time."

Jacob offered Jade a sheepish smile. "I'm sorry I had to arrest you."

Jade's mouth quirked. "You were just doing your job. I don't understand where that evidence against me came from, though."

"Officer Clemmens, the one who contacted me, was on suspension for accepting bribes, but apparently he'd hacked back into the station's system so he intercepted the missing persons inquiry. Halls paid him to fabricate the evidence to frame you. When he was arrested, he spilled everything."

"And the man on the trail, the bearded man

I shot," Jade said. "I remember him. His name was Otis Rigley. He was the man who killed my parents."

"Right," Jacob said. "Halls helped him make parole and offered him money to finish you off."

"The man with the scar on his face," Fletch interjected, "was a private investigator."

"I think I met him before. Was he working for Halls?" Jade asked.

"No, it turns out the daughter of one of Halls's victims hired him. He was onto Halls. Rigley killed him to get him off Halls's scent."

Jade ran a hand through her hair. "So it's really over, then?"

Liam and Jacob nodded, and Fletch squeezed her hand. "It's really over."

"One more thing," Jacob said. "Your commanding officer called. You're getting a commendation."

Jade shook her head. "I don't want a commendation. I'm just glad Halls can't hurt anyone else."

"He said to tell you to take some time off," Jacob added. "To come back when you're ready."

Fletch gritted his teeth. Jade was safe now. But her job was in Asheville. Would she return there now the case was solved?

JADE WAS SO relieved Halls was in jail she felt like sobbing. He had killed her partner and all those couples. And that private investigator. And his own wife…

"Are you okay?" Fletch asked gruffly.

She blinked back tears. "Just grateful Halls will pay for what he did."

"Me, too." Fletch looked down at his hands, then back at her, his expression more closed than it was before his brothers had come in.

"Fletch," Liam said. "There's more. That notebook and map you gave me. We got a hit on fingerprints."

"Yeah, whose were they?" Fletch asked.

"Guy named Barry Inman," Liam replied. "He was suing Whistler Hospital claiming negligence. According to the lawyer handling the claim for the hospital, Inman became unhinged after his wife's death. Lawsuit was thrown out the day before the hospital fire."

"Apparently Inman threatened revenge," Jacob said. "We have a BOLO out for him now to bring him in for questioning."

Hope flared in Fletch's eyes. They finally had a possible lead on his father's killer.

"Will keep you posted," Liam said. Then he and Jacob left the room.

Jade tugged the sheet over her. "That's good news."

Fletch shrugged. "It's a start."

A heartbeat of silence fell between them.

Fletch's earlier question about her relationships taunted her.

He cleared his throat. "Congratulations on the commendation. I guess you're anxious to return to your job."

Jade twisted the sheet between her fingers. She'd thought they were on the verge of some kind of revelation about their feelings. But he seemed to be shutting down.

Was he ready for her to leave town so he could go on with his life?

"I think I'll accept my boss's offer to take some time off. It's been a long few weeks."

"That's understandable. You've been through a lot." He stood. "I guess I should let you rest."

Jade watched him walk to the door with her heart in her throat. Was it really over between them?

Keep running, Jade. One foot in front of the other. You have to escape him.

That's what she'd told herself over and over when Halls and his hired gunman had been after her.

But she wasn't running from them any longer.

She'd had the courage to face her attacker. She had to have the courage to run toward what she wanted now.

And she didn't want her relationship with Fletch to end.

He opened the door and started to walk out,

and she called his name. When he turned and looked at her, longing burned in his eyes.

"You asked me a question before your brothers came in," she said softly.

He released the doorknob and closed the door. "I did. But you didn't answer."

"Do you still want to know?"

A tiny smile flickered in his eyes. "Yeah, I do."

Her heart fluttered. "I have feelings for a man," she said quietly.

His eyes twinkled, although uncertainty flickered there, as well. "You do?"

"Yes, but I'm not sure he feels the same way."

He walked back over to the bed and looked down at her. "Tell me about him."

She tugged his hand in hers. "He's brave and courageous. He rescues people in trouble," she said. "He rescued me."

Fletch sank into the chair beside her bed again, then leaned toward her, his lips inches from hers. "Actually, it's the other way around. You rescued him."

Hope overrode her insecurities. Maybe she wasn't making a fool out of herself. "From what?"

"From living a life without love."

Another heartbeat of silence stretched between them. "You have my love if you want it," she said in a raw whisper.

Fletch brushed his lips over hers. "I want it,

Jade. I want you." He kissed her tenderly, then placed his hand over his chest. "I love you with all my heart."

Hers burst with happiness. In the midst of a terrible blizzard, she and Fletch had found each other. They'd survived the elements and a murderer together.

No more uncertainty or holes in the past.

Now they could build a future based on the truth and on their love.

And maybe…she'd use her skills to help him track down his father's killer.

* * * * *

Look for more books in
USA TODAY *bestselling author*
Rita Herron's
Badge of Honor miniseries later in 2020.

And don't miss the previous book in the series:

Mysterious Abduction

Available now from Harlequin Intrigue!

Get 4 FREE REWARDS!

We'll send you 2 FREE Books plus 2 FREE Mystery Gifts.

PRESENTS

Indian Prince's Hidden Son
USA TODAY BESTSELLING AUTHOR
LYNNE GRAHAM

PRESENTS

The Greek's One-Night Heir
USA TODAY BESTSELLING AUTHOR
NATALIE ANDERSON

Harlequin Presents books feature the glamorous lives of royals and billionaires in a world of exotic locations, where passion knows no bounds.

FREE Value Over **$20**

YES! Please send me 2 FREE Harlequin Presents novels and my 2 FREE gifts (gifts are worth about $10 retail). After receiving them, if I don't wish to receive any more books, I can return the shipping statement marked "cancel." If I don't cancel, I will receive 6 brand-new novels every month and be billed just $4.55 each for the regular-print edition or $5.80 each for the larger-print edition in the U.S., or $5.49 each for the regular-print edition or $5.99 each for the larger-print edition in Canada. That's a savings of at least 11% off the cover price! It's quite a bargain! Shipping and handling is just 50¢ per book in the U.S. and $1.25 per book in Canada.* I understand that accepting the 2 free books and gifts places me under no obligation to buy anything. I can always return a shipment and cancel at any time. The free books and gifts are mine to keep no matter what I decide.

Choose one: ☐ **Harlequin Presents Regular-Print** (106/306 HDN GNWY) ☐ **Harlequin Presents Larger-Print** (176/376 HDN GNWY)

Name (please print)

Address   Apt. #

City   State/Province   Zip/Postal Code

Mail to the **Reader Service:**
IN U.S.A.: P.O. Box 1341, Buffalo, NY 14240-8531
IN CANADA: P.O. Box 603, Fort Erie, Ontario L2A 5X3

Want to try 2 free books from another series? Call 1-800-873-8635 or visit www.ReaderService.com.

*Terms and prices subject to change without notice. Prices do not include sales taxes, which will be charged (if applicable) based on your state or country of residence. Canadian residents will be charged applicable taxes. Offer not valid in Quebec. This offer is limited to one order per household. Books received may not be as shown. Not valid for current subscribers to Harlequin Presents books. All orders subject to approval. Credit or debit balances in a customer's account(s) may be offset by any other outstanding balance owed by or to the customer. Please allow 4 to 6 weeks for delivery. Offer available while quantities last.

Your Privacy—The Reader Service is committed to protecting your privacy. Our Privacy Policy is available online at www.ReaderService.com or upon request from the Reader Service. We make a portion of our mailing list available to reputable third parties that offer products we believe may interest you. If you prefer that we not exchange your name with third parties, or if you wish to clarify or modify your communication preferences, please visit us at www.ReaderService.com/consumerchoice or write to us at Reader Service Preference Service, P.O. Box 9062, Buffalo, NY 14240-9062. Include your complete name and address.

HP20R

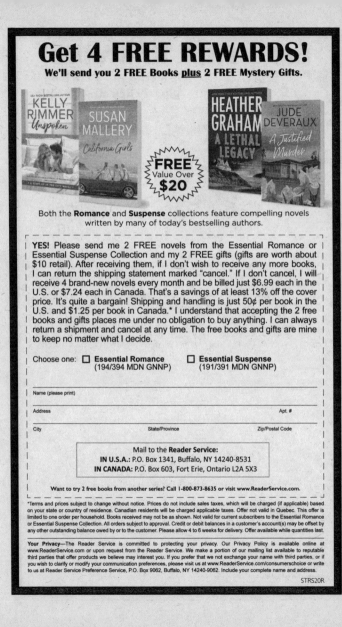

Get 4 FREE REWARDS!

We'll send you 2 FREE Books plus 2 FREE Mystery Gifts.

KELLY RIMMER
Unspoken

SUSAN MALLERY
California Girls

FREE
Value Over
$20

HEATHER GRAHAM
A LETHAL LEGACY

JUDE DEVERAUX
A Justified Murder

Both the **Romance** and **Suspense** collections feature compelling novels
written by many of today's bestselling authors.

YES! Please send me 2 FREE novels from the Essential Romance or
Essential Suspense Collection and my 2 FREE gifts (gifts are worth about
$10 retail). After receiving them, if I don't wish to receive any more books,
I can return the shipping statement marked "cancel." If I don't cancel, I will
receive 4 brand-new novels every month and be billed just $6.99 each in the
U.S. or $7.24 each in Canada. That's a savings of at least 13% off the cover
price. It's quite a bargain! Shipping and handling is just 50¢ per book in the
U.S. and $1.25 per book in Canada.* I understand that accepting the 2 free
books and gifts places me under no obligation to buy anything. I can always
return a shipment and cancel at any time. The free books and gifts are mine
to keep no matter what I decide.

Choose one: ☐ **Essential Romance**   ☐ **Essential Suspense**
                    (194/394 MDN GNNP)   (191/391 MDN GNNP)

Name (please print)

Address   Apt. #

City   State/Province   Zip/Postal Code

> Mail to the **Reader Service:**
> **IN U.S.A.:** P.O. Box 1341, Buffalo, NY 14240-8531
> **IN CANADA:** P.O. Box 603, Fort Erie, Ontario L2A 5X3

Want to try 2 free books from another series? Call 1-800-873-8635 or visit www.ReaderService.com.

STRS20R

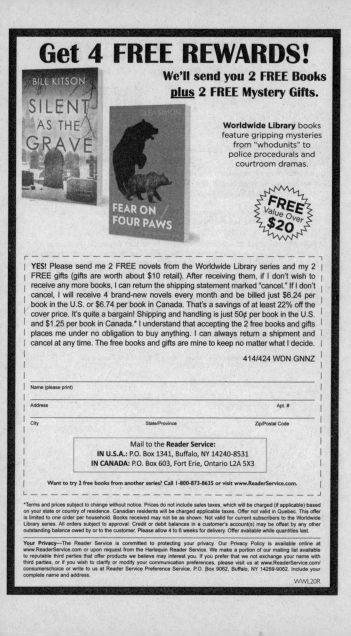